MISRULE BRITANNIA

A journalist sent to cover the outbreak of civil war in a former colony, where the discovery of oil has led to a breakaway movement in one province, is quickly plunged into the conflicts and corruption of a divided and underdeveloped country. While he reports on public events his personal life is transformed by his encounter with the young woman of mixed race who becomes his photographer. From her he learns how difficult it is to think and act rationally in a society where religion still has powerful influence. And when he gets close to the charismatic leader of the revolt he sees how personality can determine political decisions.

The story may sound familiar, but the ex-colony is Britain and the journalist from the former imperial power is Japanese – in an 'alternative history' scenario where eastern Asia has been given the historical role of western Europe. Seeing a world stage on which the actors have changed costumes may give the reader a new perspective on real events in recent decades. The pains and pleasures experienced by the individual characters are of a kind that can be seen at any time, in any place.

Misrule Britannia

Derek Walker

All characters in this book are fictitious and any resemblance to real persons, living or dead, is purely coincidental.

ISBN 978-1-84753-968-7

Typesetting and design by Christine Price

Published 2006 by Derek Walker

Dorset Square, London NW1

Distribution at www.lulu.com

ABOUT THE AUTHOR

DEREK WALKER was born and grew up in Northern Ireland. He graduated at the London School of Economics and since then has continued to live in London. For ten years he worked as a journalist, and in 1966 became Education Officer of the newly-formed Voluntary Committee on Overseas Aid and Development. When VCOAD was dissolved in 1977 he became Director of the Centre for World Development Education (later renamed Worldaware) which took over its educational work. In 1998 he was appointed OBE.

Since retiring from Worldaware in 2000 he has written five novels. *Misrule Britannia* is the second to be published and a third will shortly follow it.

The original idea for *Misrule Britannia* came to him when he was sitting at the Cabinet table in 10 Downing Street on the day the Biafran civil war in Nigeria ended. He had been summoned there with other representatives of Aid organizations for a consultation with Harold Wilson.

His first novel, *Fond Delusions*, tells the story of a young idealist who goes from grammar school in 1950s Northern Ireland to the LSE and then, when his first love affair fails, is caught up in the Algerian war as a Foreign Legionnaire. He takes part in the invasion of Suez, but eventually returns to London and begins a new life.

TO BE PUBLISHED

IN FEBRUARY 2007

SENSE AND SENSUALITY tells how a young asylum-seeker from Kazakhstan is given a bird's-eye view of the history of Western civilization by the head of a London-based think-tank for whom she does a Russian translation. He is working on a paper pointing out lessons the UN could learn from its failure to prevent genocide in Darfur. And when he reflects on his private life he thinks that a 21st Century Jane Austen might observe: 'It is a truth universally acknowledged that a single man, thirteen years divorced, must be in want of a woman to share his bed.'

CHAPTER 1

The tip of my ballpoint skidded across the page as, for the hundredth time, the train jolted to a standstill. (It was in the days before laptops, when one computer needed a small room to accommodate it.) Smoke from the labouring locomotive drifted past the carriage window, and I rubbed the glass with the heel of my hand to clear it of condensation. I could see the menacing shapes of howitzers squatting under their tarpaulins on the flat-cars of a train halted on the parallel track, and I wondered if they might be the guns manned by the five young officers facing me across the compartment – all artillerymen by their badges.

My newspaper's local correspondent had been very lucky – or had pulled some useful strings – to get me a seat on this northbound train, with half of the army moving to the same destination. He was a lecturer at the university in the capital city, who wrote an occasional piece for my paper when there was anything worth reporting from this normally very un-newsworthy ex-colonial territory. But now that the place seemed to be on the verge of civil war the Foreign Editor had sent me ten thousand miles to cover it at first hand. There's nothing like a spot of violence to justify the price of an air fare.

I'd spent the previous evening getting a hurried briefing from the local stringer on this, to me, totally unfamiliar country. Until twenty-four hours before it had meant little more than a half-remembered school geography lesson: chief exports – wool, coal and iron-ore, or was it fish? I recalled a textbook picture of a huge temple with spires and painted windows and elaborate stone carvings. Now the natives were going to start killing each other, largely because of the oil that one of our companies had discovered beneath their territorial waters. (I'd have to be careful not to use that word "natives" in my copy. It had gone out of favour because of the racist connotations given to it by the semi-literate.)

Once again the train jolted into motion and a young officer who had been dozing lurched forward, awakening just in time to prevent himself from sliding to the floor. His comrades laughed at his discomfiture in the loud, raucous manner of their country. I wished that I could understand what they were saying, since their conversation might have provided some "human interest" for my report, and I was well aware that the readers would appreciate a little light relief to the indigestible details of politicians with unpronounceable names. Still, they'd have to have those details if they were going to follow what was happening over the next few days.

I peered out at the passing countryside with renewed interest, now that we'd left behind the depressing shanty towns that clustered around the capital city. They made it look like every other developing country I'd visited – except that, somehow, the huts made of plywood boxes with palm-leaf roofs I'd seen in Pelembang didn't depress me as much as these hovels of tarred timber and corrugated iron rusting in the cold northern rain. But now that we were out among the hills and trees, speeding through a patchwork of tiny cultivated fields, the alien landscape seemed more welcoming in spite of the drizzle.

I turned my attention back to the notebook resting on my knee and began to write:

> *Last night the National Assembly met in the capital, London, to discuss the rapidly worsening crisis. Prime Minister John Serjeant faced fierce criticism from the opposition People's Democratic Party for his handling of the situation in Scotland, the disaffected northern province. He was even accused by veteran leader of the independence movement and founder of his own party, Edward Shrub, of inflaming the army mutiny which has brought this country to the verge of civil war.*
>
> *Four days ago Serjeant ordered the arrest of the newly-emerged leader of the break-away Scottish Covenant League, Andrew Knox, for allegedly trying to incite the garrison in Edinburgh, the provincial capital, to mutiny. A mob rescued Knox from the city's ancient Tolbooth Prison, and when the garrison, men of a Scottish regiment, were ordered to disperse the rioters they refused to leave their barracks in the castle.*
>
> *Immediately Serjeant ordered two other regiments to Edinburgh, to disarm the mutineers, one from the north of England (largest province of the British Republic) and the other from the north of Scotland. The latter regiment is composed mainly of highlanders recruited from remote mountain regions, who speak a different language from the men in Edinburgh and were apparently expected to have little sympathy with them.*

However, Prime Minister Serjeant seems to have made the double mistake of doubting their reliability while depending on their loyalty. He sent an English Lieutenant-Colonel from London by plane to take command of the operation; but the Scottish colonel was affronted by this slight to his rank and refused to accept the Englishman's orders. So the regiment marched into Edinburgh and joined forces with the mutineers. When the English regiment came up next day it prudently decided to dig in on the outskirts of the city and await reinforcements.

In the Assembly yesterday Opposition leader Mark Gowrie urged restraint in the interests of national unity. He proposed that the mutinous troops should be offered an amnesty, and that a constitutional conference should be arranged to discuss a federal solution. But this proposal was rejected outright by the Prime Minister.

Mr. Serjeant argued that the crisis was all the work of a handful of militants who represented nobody but themselves. His government had been democratically elected to govern, and that was what it intended to do. Whatever force might be needed to disarm the mutineers would be used, and law and order would be restored in the Scottish province.

The Prime Minister received strong support from Anne Cobbleigh, leader of the Christian Heritage Party, a minority group in the governing coalition. There are known to be strong Buddhist elements in the Scottish break-away movement (Japanese missionary influence was strong in Scotland) and the CHP was responsible for recent legislation banning non-Christians from government jobs.

When the Assembly voted in the early hours of this morning the CHP combined with Mr. Serjeant's British People's League to overwhelm the Opposition. With all but two of the fourteen members of the moderate Scottish People's League voting with the government, the issue was never really in doubt.

So now it looks as if the gun, which has been absent from politics in Britain since the granting of independence by Japan eleven years ago, will decide the outcome. Units based in the southern provinces of England and Wales constitute the overwhelming majority of the armed forces, but because of the country's poor communications network it may be several days before they can all reach the northern town of Newcastle upon Tyne, where a punitive expeditionary force is being assembled.

The rain clouds had begun to drift away, and through the window I caught a glimpse of a mellow stone tower brooding over a cluster of little houses. I presumed it must be a Christian temple, and its photogenic qualities prompted me to wonder whether a photographer would be waiting for me in Newcastle, as promised.

Our British correspondent, John Marlowe, had arranged for me to be met in Newcastle by a man who would act as guide, interpreter and driver for the rest of the journey.

"If anything needs to be fixed, Bernie will fix it," he'd said.

I hoped he was right. One of the things that Bernie was going to arrange was a local photographer to accompany us to the battlefield – or whatever it was that lay ahead. I wasn't sure if any of the international news agencies had put a photographer in yet, and it would be quite a coup if the *Nagoya Guardian* could get some exclusive pictures.

The train began to slow down again and one of the soldiers stood up and opened the window to look out. A wisp of smoke from the engine drifted in and the smell took me straight back to my childhood and the days when we still had steam trains in Japan. The town where I grew up was a railway junction, and I often walked to the bottom of the road to watch the Asahikawa express go thundering across the bridge, its mantle of smoke swirling behind it and – if the wind was from the south – filling my nostrils with the acrid, exciting smell of travel to distant places. Petrol fumes have never had the same effect on me.

It was evening and the light had almost gone when we finally clanked and creaked our way into the station at Newcastle. I climbed down stiffly on to the platform, my muscles cramped from sitting so long in one position. There were few civilians around, apart from the railway staff in their Eastern-style uniforms. I picked my way through piles of kitbags towards the entrance hall, which was built in the rather flamboyant style that characterized Japanese architecture about seventy years ago, when we were still confident of our imperial destiny.

Suddenly I saw my own name, printed in red letters on a large sheet of white paper. The paper was being held aloft by a stocky man with a round, close-cropped head of black hair and a red face that was puckered with intense concentration as he scanned the approaching stream of travellers. The moment I turned in his direction he noticed me and began to walk towards me.

"Mr. Hashimoto?" he asked.

"Yes," I replied. "And you will be Bernie Samuel?"

He bowed. "The same, in person. Have a good journey then?" His pronunciation of Japanese was good, but his voice had a curious, nasal intonation. He took my suitcase and I followed him out into the station forecourt, which was crammed with military trucks.

"We're parked around the corner," said Bernie. "Never get out through that lot." I followed him to a side street where we found a dirty, but fairly new Toyota Rough Rider, on the windscreen of which was a hand-printed label in red lettering which said (in English) "International Press".

"Jump in," said Bernie, opening the door and heaving my suitcase into the back. "We haven't far to go. I've booked you into the Kyoto Hotel. It's smaller than the Republic, but the food's better."

On the short journey he asked me a few polite but searching questions about myself – where I came from, what I did, how much I earned. The answers seemed to satisfy him, for he grinned at me as we got out of the Rough Rider and said, "You leave it to me, captain. We'll find the big news, wherever it is."

I enquired about the photographer. He would be coming up from York, the regional capital, in the morning, said Bernie. It had been a bit difficult to find one, since there was only a single newspaper in the North and its man was fully occupied. But he'd been on to an agency that did commercial work – advertisements, tourist brochures, that kind of thing – and they'd promised to send their best cameraman. Bernie was fairly certain they had only two, but he'd seen some of their work and it was good. I was very doubtful. Press photography was a lot different, and even more so under war conditions. Maybe it hadn't been such a good idea after all.

I finished writing my story before going to bed. It would be time enough to send it off in the morning. That was one advantage of reporting from a place that was nine hours behind Otsu Mean Time.

The rain had cleared next morning and there were even a few weak shafts of sunlight flickering between the scurrying grey clouds when I looked through the window at breakfast. Bernie had been up before me, getting petrol. There was likely to be a shortage, with all the military vehicles around, he said.

We were just finishing breakfast when a tall girl in a long, black, woollen cloak walked into the dining-room. There were, I suppose, a dozen people in the room and every one of them must have looked in her direction the moment she crossed the threshold.

She was a little above average height for a European woman, and a halo of glistening black curls gave her added stature. But it was her face that immediately drew my eyes – and everyone else's. She wasn't beautiful in any of the conventional patterns of feminine beauty, either Eastern or Western. Her face was a shade long, perhaps, and her mouth was wide and full, but the proportions were pleasing. It was her eyes, however, that made the face so compelling. They were widely spaced, large and dark, fringed with long lashes and flashing with vitality.

Her skin was not the usual Western blend of pink and white, or grey. It was a light, creamy brown in colour. And her nose, now that I looked at it, was decidedly flat. I guessed that she was no more than part British – almost certainly an Aiseuropean.

The girl came towards our table and I rose to greet her. She smiled, with so much warmth and sweetness and – so it seemed to me – sincerity that I felt I had just been awarded a prize.

"Mr. Hashimoto?" she asked, and, looking at Bernie, "Mr. Samuel?"

"Yes," I replied, wondering what her business with me could be.

"I'm Miranda Medway," she said. "I've come from Northern Visual Services, to do the photographs for you."

For a moment I stared at her, stupidly, and I saw the sparkle in her eyes begin to fade. She seemed to know what I was thinking. A woman press photographer in Japan would have been unusual, but here, in a developing country, where 'women's rights' were a novelty introduced only in the past decade, the idea would never have occurred to me.

"You realize this could be very dangerous?" I asked. "We're going to keep right up close to the fighting, if there is any."

Her dark brown eyes looked at me very seriously. "I can only die once – the same as you," she said. I laughed, and the sparkle came back into her eyes.

"Please sit down," I said. "Have you had breakfast yet?"

"I don't usually eat breakfast," she replied, "but I'd love a cup of tea."

She undid the clasp at her neck and slipped off the long cloak, revealing the kind of figure that used to haunt my adolescent daydreams. Her measurements would not have won an Eastern beauty contest, but in my eyes they were perfection. Her breasts were big and firm beneath her white Eastern-style sweater, and when she turned to lay her cloak over a chair I caught my breath at the symmetry of the line from waist to thigh revealed in the swirl of her calf-length black skirt.

I know that the sudden change in my attitude would have merited the scorn of *Nagoya Guardian* readers, but I felt no guilt on that score. 'To be stirred by a woman's beauty is to pay tribute to the fountainhead of all aesthetic feelings', says Pun Poo in his *Contemplations*. And a hundred years later Wang and a score of other psychologists confirmed his intuitive belief that all appreciation of beauty has its source in human beings' primal responses to the sexually attractive characteristics of their mates. If I hadn't been influenced by this woman's face and figure it would have been a denial of her humanity as well as my own. I wouldn't pretend that those were precisely the thoughts that passed through my mind as I watched Miranda take her seat at the table that morning, but I think there was probably a split-second rehearsal of the argument as I made a cerebral gear change.

"We may have to rough it fairly often on the road. You're quite sure you don't mind that?" I asked, hoping that her answer would be "no" – and it was. Of course, she had never been on an assignment quite like this before, she said. But she had once taken pictures of an air crash in the Pennines that were used in *The Times of Europa.*

"How did you get into the picture-taking business, then?" asked Bernie. "A bit unusual for a girl, isn't it?"

"Yes, I know," she answered, smiling at him in a way that unaccountably made me feel jealous. "I think they took me on because they were too surprised to say 'no'. It started really when my uncle gave me a camera for Christmas." (Christmas, I learnt later, is a Christian festival which is marked by the exchange of gifts.) "Then I had a chance to go on a photography course that was starting at the London Technical College just when I was leaving school. Needless to say, everybody predicted that I would never get a job, but I did." She looked at me with a candour that would have disarmed any doubting prospective employer.

"You got all your gear outside, then?" asked Bernie. She nodded enthusiastically. "Right, then. We're ready to go." It was clear that any misgivings he might have had had vanished – although there was no real reason why they should have.

I decided that we had better try to find the military headquarters as soon as possible, and discover – if anyone would tell us – when the army was likely to be ready to move. It would be a good idea, I thought, to get into Scotland ahead of them and observe their advance, provided I didn't cut myself off for too long from communications. There wouldn't be much point in having a sensational story if I couldn't get to a telephone or a telex that was working, and it was unlikely that there would be many of those between Newcastle and Edinburgh.

It was late that evening before I was able to find anyone willing to talk to me at the headquarters, which was in the old Shantungese fortress (built on the site of a more ancient castle). And even then I was able to learn little, except that it would be "some days" before the deployment would be complete. Bernie's information, from less official sources, was that two regiments, the East Anglian Rifles and the London Regiment, had not even begun to move north yet, and that there was a serious shortage of ammunition of practically all calibres.

Miranda had had no difficulty in taking pictures of the troops during the day. Her main problem had been to avoid the attempts of some of them to become more closely acquainted with her. But there were no real difficulties, for the men were good-humoured and in an almost festive mood.

I had some misgivings, however, about what might happen if we ever found ourselves in the aftermath of battle. When passions were let loose in the presence of death would the restraints of civilization still operate (perhaps ‘civilization’ was the wrong word to use, since these people had their own, quite ancient, civilization) or would more primitive patterns of behaviour take over? There had been many occasions when it had happened among East Asian soldiers, even in this century. However, I put the problem out of my mind. Everybody seemed to agree that there wasn’t going to be a real battle.

The three of us sat in my bedroom that evening and reviewed the situation. If our information was accurate there would be no advance tomorrow, or possibly even on the next day. There was no story to be found sitting around here, and I was in favour of making a reconnaissance into Scotland. Miranda was enthusiastic about the idea, but Bernie feared that we might lose contact with the army if it were to move off suddenly.

“Supposing they decide to move across to Carlisle and strike up from there, to take the hairylegs by surprise?” he asked.

I looked at the map. “That’s not very likely,” I said. “There’s no railway. They couldn’t move the whole force quickly without using the railway.”

Bernie put his neat, round head on one side and ran his fingers rapidly through his short hair in a kind of scrabbling movement. “Could be right, captain. They’d never get the tanks across the Pennines.”

So we decided to head for Scotland the following day. The road was good, Bernie said (it had been built by the Japanese Army in the last century) and we should be across the Border in less than two hours. We planned to leave early in the morning, but already Bernie seemed restless to be off, and he decided to go and give the car a final check.

As he closed the door I looked at Miranda and smiled. She rewarded me with a look that made me feel I was the only person in the world of whom she was conscious.

"You're quite sure that you're ready to trust yourself to the two of us?" I asked. "There is no guarantee that we'll be able to look after you properly, once things start to liven up." I knew that what I was saying was true and I felt that I had to say it, even though the last thing I wanted was for her to change her mind.

"I take things as they come," she said. "If trouble's heading for you there's nothing you can do about it."

"You can sometimes step aside, if you see it in time."

She smiled, and I watched the slow curving of her lips and the row of even white teeth that they revealed. "Yes, but only if you think it's worth the effort," she said.

I was shocked. "That's a very pessimistic attitude for a beautiful girl with her whole life in front of her," I exclaimed.

She shook her head firmly. "I'm not beautiful."

"Well, that's not something about which I can easily argue with you," I said, "but you're the most beautiful person I've seen since I came to Britain – and for quite a long time before that. And I'm not saying it to flatter you. Beauty's much too important a subject with me for that."

She looked at me with eyes very wide open. "Do you really think so?" She seemed to be discussing the question just as objectively as I was, for I had been taken by surprise and genuinely wasn't trying to flatter her. "I've got front teeth like a rabbit," she said, smiling, and I saw that her front teeth might just possibly be described as slightly prominent.

"They're very attractive," I said, "and, anyhow, they only show when you're laughing."

"But what about the colour of my skin? It's not a proper brown. It's more like cold tea – except when I'm sick, and then it's like putty."

"I haven't seen you when you're sick," I replied, "and I hope that I won't – I mean I hope you won't be sick. But *I* think your skin is a very pleasant shade of brown. There are a lot of people at home who are just about your colour."

"Are there really?" she asked earnestly. "My great-grandmother was Shantungese, you know, and my mother's father was Japanese."

"I thought you had an interesting ancestry," I said.

"That's not what everybody would call it."

"Oh? What would other people call it?"

"They'd say I was a mongrel." She looked at me steadily and her eyes were dull.

"Apart from the fact that one mongrel can often be healthier and more reliable than a hundred pedigree prize-winners with only one grandfather between them," I said, "it would be a silly description. No nationality is pure bred, apart maybe from some of the aboriginal peoples. And their culture hasn't changed much since the Stone Age. We Japanese are as mixed a lot as you could wish to find. Why, we had our last big blood transfusion only about five hundred years ago, with the Paekchean invasion. And there have been several small ones since then. Countries that don't keep stirring the mixture are the ones that stagnate."

"Oh, I know that's true in theory," she said, not impatiently – impatience seemed to be alien to her temperament – but with a trace of resignation. "But it's what people think that matters. I suppose it's because this country is new that people bother so much about who they are and what they are."

"I don't think it's just in new countries that that happens; but maybe it's worse here. What sort of difference does it make, not being accepted as completely British?"

She leaned forward, her chin cupped in her hands, and looked at me very seriously. "It's not easy to say. I've lived most of the time in London and down there things are more mixed up and you can sort of fade into the background. But I'll never forget just before Independence – I was at school, of course. One of the girls said that when it came everybody who wasn't British would have to leave. I paid little attention, because, of course, I was British. And then another girl said, "Does that mean Miranda's going to leave?" Can you imagine what it was like, to suddenly feel that you didn't belong?

And it wasn't just that I didn't belong here. I didn't feel I was Japanese, that was for certain. Would I feel different if I was in Japan?"

"Maybe you'll find out one day," I murmured, an impossible hope flickering in my brain. "Did what happened at school make a lot of difference afterwards?"

Miranda nodded vigorously. "I'll say it did. At first I went home to my mother in floods of tears, and she tried to comfort me and tell me that nobody was going to send us away. When I was a bit calmer she said I ought to be proud of my Japanese blood. I was part of the people who had built the greatest empire the world had ever seen. But I didn't want to be part of them, I said. They were robbers and murderers and oppressors. I was British. I suppose that was the first time I felt ashamed of having East Asian blood."

"I expect it's in adolescence that most people first feel some kind of responsibility for the actions of their country – that's if they ever do," I said. "But for you it must have been much more intense, feeling the need to choose one country and reject another."

Again Miranda nodded. "It was intense all right. I joined a Camelot Club – that's the youth movement of the BPL. We wore big, round badges that were supposed to be a picture of the table at which Arthur, a legendary king of Britain, sat with his knights. The funny thing was, it looked a bit like the imperial chrysanthemum that people were busy taking down from all the public buildings. The leaders made a fuss of me, because there was all that talk about national unity, and how we were going to be one people, free and indivisible. They liked having me because our Club didn't have anyone else who wasn't pure English, let alone British. So I was chosen to carry the national flag for the Club in the local Independence Day procession. I loved it at first, but after a time I began to realize that I wasn't being treated just like anybody else. I was different. I was the prize exhibit, to show how broadminded they were. So I left."

"You must have been very perceptive for your age. How old were you then?"

"I was about fifteen by that time. And then I met this Aiseuropean boy (I hate that word, 'Aiseuropean') who was quite a lot older than me. I thought he was marvellous." She smiled, in a worldly-wise kind of a way that contradicted the innocence of her features. “Yamaga was a member of a thing called the Union of New Britons. Its aim was to stand up for the rights of Aiseuropeans, and anybody else who wasn’t a hundred per cent British. I used to go on demonstrations with them, even though I hated being stared at. I always have. But I felt I really belonged again.”

“And how did other people react to your demonstrations?”

“Well, the trouble was that, although we felt we were an oppressed minority, other people didn’t see it that way. They thought we were privileged – or had been, anyhow, until Independence. I suppose they were right, in a way. What we were really reacting against was our parents’ attitude of always pretending to be somebody else – trying to be accepted. Before Independence they wanted to be accepted as Japanese, and afterwards they wanted to be accepted as British. I still think that was wrong, but I’m not sure any longer what the alternative is.”

“Is the Union still operating?”

“No, not the way it was. It started splitting up about a year after I joined. First the Buddhists started to quarrel with the Christians, and then the majority, who were neither one nor the other, got fed up with both of them. The Christians were really more interested in integration than separate identity, and eventually they broke away and set up their own organization. After that there was a group who wanted us to be more militant – civil disobedience and that kind of thing. I went along with them for a while, even though I was very scared of what the police might do every time we had a confrontation. I got arrested once, you know.” She looked at me with eyes twinkling, as though expecting me to disbelieve her.

“Did the police hurt you?” I asked.

“No. I was lucky,” she replied. “Then Yamaga, and some of the others, said we were getting nowhere with non-violent tactics and the time had come for something more drastic. They had ideas about setting off explosions in public buildings. That was when I saw how ridiculous it was all becoming. The next step would have been killing somebody. The whole thing was getting out of proportion. We had some genuine grievances – discrimination in jobs, people being unfairly evicted, that kind of thing. But there wasn’t anything that would justify taking somebody’s life away from them. And I think our real grievance was just that we couldn't escape from being who we were, however hard we tried."

"Was there any violence? I can't remember hearing about it."

"There was one bomb, at the Independence Memorial, in Westminster, but they hadn't connected it properly and it didn't go off. After that the police moved in and rounded up a lot of people – not all of them the ones who'd done it. That was another grievance, but there was nobody left who felt like doing anything about it. Because of the bomb we'd lost practically all the support we'd had among British people."

"And what happened to Yamaga?"

"Oh, I'd split with him months before that, so I don't really know – except that the police didn't get him. I heard that he went to Europa." The inflection in her voice suggested that she was no longer interested in the subject.

"We have our problems, too," I said. "Before I came here I was covering the trouble in Southern Hokkaido."

"Oh, yes. I've heard about that. Everywhere it seems to be minorities that cause the problems."

"You could say it's the majorities that are the real cause."

"Maybe, but I'm not sure that would be fair either. Nobody seems to be able to accept being just what they are and behave in the way that goes with it. What I mean is, if you're in a majority you can afford to be tolerant and if you are it's much less likely that minorities will give you trouble. And if you're in a minority you can't expect to have the last word. If power is what you're after you've got to join the majority – if they'll let you. Bernie's lot seem to be more realistic about that than most, as far as I can see."

"Bernie's lot? Do you mean he belongs to a minority, too?"

"Didn't you know?" Her eyes were wide with surprise. "Bernie's a Jew." I was puzzled for a moment, and then I remembered.

"Oh, yes. They're a bit like the Parsees in Hindustan, aren't they? I didn't realize that there were any in Britain."

"Yes. There are quite a lot here," said Miranda. "I think it was when the Janissary Empire was breaking up that most of them came over from Europa – their ancestors, I mean. The Turks used to protect them and make use of them, but the Christians were always massacring them. But over here the Taiwanese were in control by that time and they allowed them to come. I don't really know much about history," she added, with a little shrug of her shoulders, "but I read that somewhere."

My own knowlcdgc of European history began just about that time, when the East Asians were starting to get involved. "So they've been around for two or three hundred years now? I said. "I suppose they haven't been integrated, either."

"I think some of them have. Maybe most of the ones who wanted to be – who weren't bothered about religion. But it's easier for them. After all, you didn't know by looking at him that Bernie was different."

"No. But you did."

"Maybe – but I mightn't have. His name is Jewish, too, you see."

I nodded. "That's the sort of little detail that an outsider can never hope to know, unless he lives in a country for a very long time. I hope you're going to help me not to write anything too stupid in my stories."

"I'd love to – not that I think you *would* write anything stupid." She bestowed another glowing smile on me. "If we're going to start early in the morning I'd better get to bed now. I'm never at my best unless I have enough sleep." She stood up quickly, her glorious breasts bouncing just a little under the tight sweater.

"Sleep well, then. Who knows where we may sleep tomorrow night?"

I stood at the bedroom door and watched with longing the sway of her hips as she walked along the corridor. When she reached her own door she turned and looked back at me, with a smile so sweet that I ached to follow her. Instead, I waved my hand and went back into my own room, feeling a strange mixture of loneliness and anticipation.

Since the death of my wife, three years before, there had been only two other women who had aroused the same feelings. Both of them I would willingly have taken to bed; but early in our relationships both had started dropping hints that matrimony was their goal. I suppose it would have been easy for me to have played them along for a little while, taking my pleasures in the meantime. Unfortunately, I'd grown up with the kind of conscience that gave me trouble, and I couldn't really enjoy a relationship that was grounded in deceit. So with each of them I had made my excuses and quietly slipped away.

What I hadn't been prepared to risk again was investing all my emotional capital in one person and watching it snatched away by a capricious chance. My lovely Shigenobu had been the centre of my life, but because an idiot had taken his car on the motorway after drinking too much sake, all that had ended in a pile of twisted metal. It had taken me a long time to recover from that experience. I was making no more total commitments.

Now, in Miranda I saw the possibility that I had been longing for. She was beautiful, she was intelligent, I enjoyed her company and she seemed to enjoy mine. Perhaps her own rootlessness and apparent alienation from the community in which she lived might make her ready to accept a temporary relationship, and to enjoy each day for what it brought, rather than for any promise it might give of future permanence. As I fell asleep remembering the movement of her hips, I had the thought that maybe my principles would prove flexible enough to admit just a little deceit, if her emotions should prove to be less emancipated than her intellect.

CHAPTER 2

The morning was misty when we set off for the north. I was reminded of a journey I once made from Aomori back to university at Kyoto, when I was a student. There was a mist all along the seashore from Noshiro to Sakata, and several times the ruins of castles loomed up like monsters out of the Nebuta Festival. It was the last time I made that particular journey. On the next occasion when I visited my boyhood home in Southern Hokkaido I went by air.

We sat all three in the front seat, and the warm softness of Miranda's hip and thigh pressed against my own made me oblivious of the chill morning air. She was wearing a fawn sweater with a high, turned-over collar behind which she now sank her chin for warmth, so that she looked like some large-eyed animal of the forest peeping out of its burrow. For a while my thoughts were not really on the work ahead of us. Then Bernie started to whistle, interrupting my train of thought, and I came back to reality.

The villages we passed through were poor-looking places, though the cottages were, in the main, solidly built of stone. But I saw little sign of Eastern technology. Tractors, bicycles, electricity, even wire fences, were not in evidence. And I thought that many of the children we saw on the road, clean and neat though they were, looked inadequately dressed for the climate.

"Do all the children go to school?" I asked.

"In theory, yes," said Bernie, "up to – twelve is it?"

"Yes, twelve," Miranda agreed.

"But what really happens," he went on, "is that about half of them go all the time and the rest go when they can be spared from doing other things. And some don't go at all, because they live too far away from a school – see what I mean? When I was a lad we lived right in the middle of town, so I never had an excuse for staying away. It was always my older brother that got kept at home to look after the stall – in the market, you know. My old father used to say, 'Bernie, my boy, make the most of your chances. Education is the one useful thing you can get that nobody can ever take away from you.' I didn't see it that way at the time, but he was right, of course. Now I wish I'd been able to go to the high school; but there were five of us youngsters and the old man hadn't got the money – see what I mean?"

We went on talking about the education system until suddenly, at a bend in the road, I caught a glimpse of what seemed to be a walled town lying ahead of us.

"Where are we coming to now?" I asked.

"This'll be Berwick on Tweed," said Bernie

"It looks as if it still has a wall round it," I remarked.

"Yes. Most of the old wall is still standing," said Miranda. "It should be quite a tourist attraction, but not many tourists come as far as this. Farther south, ending up near to Newcastle, there's still quite a lot of the old wall that the Romans built right across the country – like the Great Wall from the Ala Shan to the Gulf of Liaotung, only not as long, of course. You see, I do know a little bit of Asian history." She smiled and drew up her head, stretching her long, graceful neck.

There was no sign of unusual activity in the town and it looked rather a sleepy place, although Bernie said it was very busy on market days. We passed through without stopping, and then Bernie announced that we were in Scotland. However often I pass from one country or province to another (and I've done it a great many times) I still expect to see some immediate change, but I very rarely do. On this occasion we had been driving for about half-an-hour when I saw the first sign of difference, and it was quite a striking one. From the centre of a small town which we were approaching I saw arising the wooden roof of a rather stumpy pagoda.

"A pagoda!" I exclaimed. "That's the first I've seen in Britain – though I know there are several in London."

"There are quite a lot of Buddhists in this part of the country," said Miranda.

"Used to be a lot of missionaries, too – monks and that," Bernie added, "but most of them have gone now. Funny thing, isn't it? – Buddhists have monks and Christians have monks, but us Jews, we don't have monks. Not that we haven't got some very religious fellows."

"Are there very many monks – Christian monks, I mean – in Britain?" I asked.

"Thousands of them," said Miranda. "But they say there used to be a lot more."

“I’ve heard,” said Bernie, “there was a time when one fellow out of every five was a monk or a priest. Nowadays it’s more like one in a hundred. That’s why the population’s going up so fast. There are more fellows in circulation – see what I mean?”

“From what I’ve heard,” said Miranda, laughing, “it didn’t always make much difference whether they were monks or not.”

We passed through the town, a place called Dunbar, which was on the sea-coast, and saw little else of interest till we again struck the coast at Cockenzie. I noticed that a lot of the land now looked like rich arable, and the houses were numerous, but mostly small and roughly built. Bernie said we were getting close to Edinburgh, and before very long we saw the outskirts of the city – the familiar huddles of shacks made of planks, corrugated iron, canvas and whatever else the squatters could lay hands on. In the distance I glimpsed the great black mass of a castle lowering over the town. It would certainly make a perfect target – and a perfect gun platform. As we turned into a fine, modern street, evidently built towards the end of the colonial era, a military scout car appeared and drew alongside us. It contained three soldiers in dark green battledress and helmets, who signalled us to stop.

We drew in to the kerb and the scout car pulled in ahead of us. As a sergeant, carrying a sub-machine-gun, jumped out and walked back towards us Bernie wound down his window. The man said something in English, sounding polite, I thought. Bernie replied and then turned to me, saying, “He wants your papers.” I pulled out everything that might be relevant and handed it over, and the sergeant scrutinized each document in turn. Then he passed them all back to me.

“I would like you to accompany us to our headquarters,” he said, speaking in slow and careful Japanese. I consented eagerly.

“Here’s a stroke of luck,” I said as we pulled out behind the scout car. “We may even get a chance to talk to some of the leaders.”

“More likely they’re just going to commandeer the Rough Rider,” said Bernie, gloomily. “See what I mean?” He nodded towards about a dozen light trucks and private cars lined up in a side street, apparently under guard. “I should have thought of that before I drove in here in broad daylight, like a bus to the Blaydon Races. She’ll make a lovely scout car for the hairylegs.”

"He didn't sound as if he was going to take the car," said Miranda.

I put my hand on her knee and squeezed it gently, "Bernie's feeling pessimistic because we haven't had lunch yet," I said.

We drove up a steep street that led to the Castle entrance. Two sentries with rifles guarded the end of the bridge that led to the gateway and I caught a glimpse of a machine-gun on the battlements above. For a couple of minutes while the sergeant talked to an officer at the gate, we waited with our engine running, and then we were allowed to drive under the grim portcullis.

There was little time to take stock of our surroundings, but this place was certainly the nearest I had come to my dreams of the explorer, Kusunoke, when he came upon the walled town of San Gimignano with its forest of high towers, in his journey through Southern Europa. But although the setting might be romantic, the activity going on seemed to be very realistic. I saw a group of about fifty men in civilian clothing, but each wearing a blue armband with a white X on it, drilling with rifles. And in another open space a civilian truck was being fitted with steel plates, to turn it into a makeshift armoured car.

We stopped the car and waited while the sergeant went inside a rather ugly, utilitarian office block of Japanese construction. A few minutes later he returned and opened the car door, addressing himself directly to me, "The Chief will see you. Follow me."

"Can my photographer come, too?" I asked, pointing to Miranda. "I would like to have a picture of the Chief."

He looked doubtful for a moment, but then nodded his head. "Bring the camera."

Bernie said, "I'll stay here and keep an eye on the car."

As we followed the sergeant into the dark, panelled hallway I asked, "Who is the Chief?"

He turned his head in surprise. "Mr. Knox. Who else?"

We were led into a long room that looked as if it might previously have been an officers' mess. On the far wall hung a huge map of northern Britain and below it, at a long table, sat two men, with a third standing behind them. The young officer who was standing wore the now familiar dark green battledress. The smaller of the two men at the table, who had black hair streaked with grey and bright, piercing eyes, also wore battledress. But the big man – who was quite clearly 'the Chief' – was wearing a brown, Eastern-style jacket and, when he rose to greet us, I saw that beneath it he wore a multi-coloured pleated skirt, with a fur pouch hanging down in front. (This 'kilt', I was shortly to learn, was the traditional garb of the people who lived in the northern, Highland part of the country.) He was a huge man, over six feet in height, with a great stomach from which the kilt hung like a bell tent. His head was small and pointed, with close-cropped, ginger hair and he had a small ginger moustache. A second chin had formed to cushion the first, and the curious blend of features was completed by a hooked nose and eyes that seemed fish-like behind thick, horn-rimmed spectacles.

When he spoke his voice was surprisingly light for such a large man; and his Japanese was faultless. "Welcome to Scotland, young man. You've come a long way. And who is the young lady?"

"My photographer. I hope that before we leave you will allow us the honour of taking some photographs," I replied.

"Yes, indeed. Charming." He leered at Miranda. "Pray be seated."

The sergeant brought us chairs.

"This is my Chief of Staff, Major Johnston," said Knox, with an expansive wave of his hand towards the seated officer, who nodded curtly by way of greeting.

"We are especially pleased to have the representative of such a distinguished journal in our midst," Knox continued. "You are the first foreign reporter to find his way to our newly-independent country." Although his Japanese was excellent I noticed that he had a fondness for old-fashioned phraseology that made him sound like an elderly mayor at a school speech day.

I expressed surprise that I should be the first to arrive and he replied, "Yes, indeed. And we will ensure that you have every facility you may require. In Scotland we believe most ardently in the freedom of the Press; and we have no secrets to hide from the world."

Johnston cleared his throat immediately. "Ay… there are certain military matters which we wouldn't want to have disclosed prematurely, of course," he said, in a soft, sing-song voice.

"Of course," I said.

Knox smiled benignly. "Major Johnston very rightly reminds us of the unhappy condition in which we find ourselves – a state of war. And I'm sure the English generals are all diligent readers of the *Nagoya Guardian*, so we wouldn't want to give them an unfair advantage, would we? If you would just be kind enough to let Captain Mackie cast his eye over any report before it is transmitted – simply as a precaution." He indicated the young officer who was standing by the map.

"Certainly," I said. "And since you suggest that there may be action ahead, can I ask to be allowed to accompany your troops?"

"I don't see why not." He looked questioningly at Johnston, who said nothing. "Yes. You may well be the first to chronicle a glorious page in the annals of Scotland." Then he leaned his great weight forward on the table and looked at me earnestly. "But already there is news for your readers – news that all the world must know."

I took out my notebook and ballpoint.

Knox nodded his head approvingly and continued, "This morning Scotland once again became a free and independent nation. With my own hands I raised our ancient banner of Saint Andrew above this castle. Captain Mackie will give you a copy of the Declaration of Independence. Scotland seeks only to control her own destiny, and to use her own great natural resources for the benefit of all her people. And Almighty God has been pleased to bestow on her great wealth, which has been stored up against this hour of need."

I saw Johnston's head give a slight twitch at the words 'Almighty God'. Knox must have seen it too, for he immediately added, "Freedom of worship for every man will be the cornerstone of our constitution, and all religions will be given equal respect."

Johnston must be a Buddhist, I thought.

Knox continued, "Peace is our aim, but we are ready to defend our freedom with our lives." He paused and looked at me very hard. I felt that he was expecting me to applaud – or perhaps he saw in my notebook the million readers of the *Guardian.*

“Has a provisional government been set up?” I asked.

He beamed at me. “Yes, indeed, young man. A group of forty elected town and county councillors from every part of the country have taken up the reins of government until a constituent assembly can be called together.” He paused and then added, “I have been prevailed upon to become Prime Minister and Acting Head of State. It is a heavy burden, but I accept it humbly and willingly, in the service of all that I hold most dear.” I noticed that Captain Mackie was looking at him admiringly – clearly a convert. Johnston’s dark little face showed no sign of emotion.

“Captain Mackie will let you have the list of the ministerial posts,” said Knox. “And now I am sure you will appreciate that we have a great many things to be attending to.”

“You have been very generous with your time,” I replied. “I hope we may be able to talk again before long.”

He beamed at me once more. “You mentioned photographs. If you would really like some I can spare another minute or two.”

Miranda had her flash-gun rigged up in a matter of seconds and took several shots of him in front of the map, and a couple in attitudes of consultation with Major Johnston. Then he insisted on having one taken with me, his arm around my shoulder. I felt very foolish – and could see that Miranda was taking a mischievous delight in my embarrassment. But then I reflected that the picture might find a use in my autobiography, if I ever got around to writing one.

When the interview was finally concluded I hastened to prepare my story for Captain Mackie’s approval. It could still be in time to make the front page. (I later learned that it had been printed near the foot of Page Four, under the headline *Independence move in North Britain.*)

I was anxious to convey some hint that the Scots were likely to seize the military initiative, but wondered how I could word it in a way that would escape Mackie’s blue pencil. Eventually I wrote: *A dynamic leader like Knox is unlikely to sit idly waiting for his enemies to attack. He is the kind of man who can be expected to do the unexpected.* It got past – but then I wondered what the Foreign Editor would make of it.

As we parted from him Mackie said, “If you want to move with the army be ready to leave at any moment, day or night.”

When we rejoined Bernie we found that he, too, had been making good use of his time. As well as having bought enough food for a substantial lunch, he had picked up a lot of interesting information.

The North English Regiment had put one battalion into the Port of Leith, where they had barricaded themselves in the docks, while the other battalion was stationed to the west, straddling the roads and railway lines to Glasgow and Falkirk. Evidently the plan was to cut off the Scots’ retreat when they were attacked by the force advancing from the south and east. But the Scottish troops were getting ready to move. They had commandeered practically everything on wheels in the city; and they had enlisted and armed several hundred volunteers, mainly ex-soldiers.

“It looks as if they’ve got some pretty clever fellows running the show,” said Bernie.

We spent the afternoon in the Castle, watching as much of the preparations as we were permitted to see. Engines were being tested, trucks loaded with ammunition and batches of civilian volunteers put through their drill. Later on officers started talking to the men by companies, but we were not allowed to get close to these briefing sessions.

I was interested to see men of the North Scottish Regiment wearing kilts below their battledress blouses. Miranda pointed out that the kilts of each company had a different pattern or ‘tartan’. In the Highlands, she explained, each clan was distinguished by its own tartan. Bernie added the information that companies of the regiment tended to be made up of men of the same clan.

The day had become overcast, with a light drizzle, and when we heard the sound of an aero engine it was a long time before we caught sight of the plane, which was then banking over Leith. It was small and single-engined, and Bernie later learnt that it was an Air Force trainer. The machine-gunners waited eagerly for it to come within range, but it flew off to the south.

When we had had our evening meal, brought to us from the cookhouse on Captain Mackie’s orders, I said, “If they’re going to move out to take up position for an ambush, which is what it looks like to me, I think they'll do it under cover of darkness. So why don't we try and get some sleep in the car before it all starts happening?"

I tucked Miranda up on the back seat, covering her with her cloak and a rug, and Bernie and I tried to make ourselves comfortable in the front. We had been travelling since early morning, and I eventually managed to doze off.

I woke up to the sound of engines starting. Bernie was already awakc. "Thcy'rc moving out," hc said.

A few minutes later Captain Mackie arrived. "The army is moving to a secret destination," he told us. "The sergeant has pasted black paper over your headlamps, so that you'll only have narrow beams of light, but the vehicle in front will have patches of fluorescent paint on it – we've put some on you, too. Keep ten meters behind it, and don't stop unless it stops."

The whole idea sounded pretty hazardous to me, especially as I remembered what Moupei had said about British standards of driving. But the young officer was clearly very excited and left us with the assurance, "Tonight you're going to see something that will go down in military history."

We drove out into the darkness, through city streets and then into the countryside. The sky must have been cloudy for there were few stars, and we could see nothing along the road but an occasional lighted window, sometimes with staring faces alarmed by the huge convoy rumbling past. Before very long the road began to climb, but apart from the change in altitude we had no idea where we were going. I was thankful that at least the rain had stopped.

The journey through the night lasted for about five hours, with only three brief halts. The road surface seemed to be good but some of the gradients were very steep. Towards the end we were descending all the way, except for a last little climb to take us over some low hills. We finally came to a halt on the outskirts of a village. The head of the convoy had already passed through it, but we were near the tail.

There was a tap on the car window and Mackie was standing outside.

"You can leave the car here and go forward on foot if you wish to," he said. "The attack will commence at 0 five hundred hours."

I looked at my watch and saw that it was nearly half-past four. "Where are we?" I asked.

"Just outside Newcastle," he replied. "If you want to follow us in by car you can move after 0 six hundred hours. But you move at your own risk. There may still be a lot of metal flying around – depends on how long they continue to resist." There was a note of victory in his voice already.

We were glad to climb out of the car, even though the air was bitterly cold, and for a minute or two we stamped our feet and stretched our arms. Then I slung my binoculars over my shoulder and Miranda hung a camera round her neck (even though there seemed little chance she would be able to take pictures for quite a long time). Bernie fetched a vacuum flask of tea that he had previously packed away.

We walked along the line of parked vehicles into the centre of the village. Lights were lit in one or two houses, but as we arrived the inhabitants were being told through loud-hailers to extinguish them and stay indoors. The tiny village inn was lighted, however, and through the doorway I caught a glimpse of Knox, Johnston and several other officers, who seemed to be setting up their headquarters there.

Files of soldiers were moving forward and then jumping down from the road into the fields on either side. The vehicles at the head of the convoy had not emptied, however. There were five lorries crammed with troops and in front of them two home-made armoured cars. Right at the head of the column I saw the unmistakable silhouettes of two Japanese-made Tartar armoured cars.

The road began to slope downward. "If we stop about here," said Bernie, "we'll probably find we're at the top of a hill when the sun comes up, and that way we ought to have a pretty good view. See what I mean?"

There was a large tree by the roadside and we stood underneath it, leaning against the trunk. To warm ourselves and pass the time we drank tea from Bernie's flask.

"It's past five o'clock," I said, peering closely at my watch.

"Look!" Miranda exclaimed, pointing to the left. A faint streak of light had appeared in the sky.

"Make you homesick for the Land of the Rising Sun, does it?" asked Bernie.

"No. I'm afraid I've always preferred sunsets, myself," I replied. "I don't much care for being up at this hour of the morning. You know, it's a funny thing, but the only book about Britain that a great many people in Japan have ever read is one called *Land of the Sunset*. It's a romantic travel book by a woman who visited this island about sixty years ago, and fell in love with it. It was popular for a long time, but I don't think it's read very much nowadays. The author might have a different view if she was here today."

"A place looks different when the sun's rising on it," said Miranda.

Minutes passed and there was still nothing to be seen or heard through the darkness ahead of us. Then suddenly the engines of the vehicles on the road just behind roared into life. One by one they moved off, now with headlamps unmasked and probing ahead of them. We watched them descend the hill at an increasing speed. The eastern sky was brightening fast and dim shapes were becoming visible all around us.

"You were right," I said to Bernie. "this is a pretty good vantage point."

We were on the top of a low hill that overlooked the town. In the murky half-light distances might be deceptive, but the black mass of building on the horizon seemed to be about two kilometres away. Far to the left there was a tapping sound, as if someone was beating with a stick on an empty wooden box.

"Rifle fire," I said. "It's started." I looked at Miranda's face and saw that her eyes were anxious, but otherwise she gave no sign of what she was thinking.

Then we heard louder reports, which could have been grenades or a light mortar, followed immediately by the unmistakable rattle of a machine-gun. A few minutes later everything was quiet again. We could now begin to pick out some of the larger buildings in the town and I trained my binoculars on a corner of the fortress, and then moved round to focus on the railway bridge. There were three heavy explosions, followed by more prolonged machine-gun fire.

Another long period of inactivity followed as the sky became brighter and a strong breeze began to blow from the direction of the coast. We heard occasional single rifle shots, but nothing more. Then the engines of the trucks on the road behind us came to life and slowly they started moving past us down the hill. Two staff cars accelerated alongside the convoy and disappeared in a cloud of dust and exhaust fumes, but I managed to catch a glimpse of Knox and Johnston, the former smiling broadly and flourishing a large cigar.

"It looks as if they've taken their objective," I said. "Let's get back to the car and follow them."

When the last of the empty lorries had rattled past we walked back through the deserted village, peered at by many faces from the cottage windows. Bernie tore the strips of black paper from the headlamps before getting inside.

"Wouldn't do to make it too obvious where we've come from," he said. "If we run into some of our fellows down there they mightn't like it. See what I mean?"

We drove into the town slowly. Our vehicle had a military appearance and we had no wish to cause alarm to any trigger-happy patrol. Miranda looked out eagerly for suitable subjects to photograph, but everything seemed to be normal – although once again we saw anxious faces at windows. Then we heard firing coming from the south side of the town, punctuated by the crump of mortar bombs, and Bernie turned the car in that direction.

Suddenly four soldiers came running out of a side street a little way ahead of us. One of them saw us and waved us to stop. He followed the gesture by aiming his rifle at our windscreen, and Bernie braked sharply. The soldier shouted something hoarsely, in English.

"He says they need the car," said Bernie, opening his door.

We climbed out as the other three soldiers came running back. Bernie was walking around the front of the vehicle to our side when I saw a look of alarm pucker up his face and he shouted, "Get down!" At almost the same instant a volley of shots rang out behind us. I flung my arms around Miranda's waist and threw her to the ground. As we lay there a second volley was fired and I saw a running soldier stumble and fall.

A rifle hit the ground with a clatter and a voice called out, and then there was no more firing. I raised my head slowly and gingerly and looked around. One of the English soldiers was standing against a wall with his hands held high above his head, and another was sitting in the gutter, clutching his left shoulder, blood trickling between his fingers. The one I had seen fall was lying very still in the road, arms and legs spreadeagled.

I looked around for the fourth but couldn't see him – and then, suddenly, I did. He was lying right beside me, on top of his rifle. A stream of blood was running along its barrel and forming a pool on the road. From behind I heard running feet and turned to see half-a-dozen Scottish soldiers – men of the Rifles, since they wore trousers rather than kilts – approaching.

"Are you all right?" I asked Miranda.

"Just a bit bruised," she replied, as I helped her to her feet. The leader of the Scots shouted something and Bernie, who had emerged from behind the bonnet, gave him an answer that seemed to satisfy him.

I saw Miranda look at the body of the Englishman lying at our feet and her eyes clouded over with horror. She put her hands on my shoulders and began to cry, silently but with great convulsive sobs that I felt through her tightly clutching fingers. I drew her close to me and held her firmly for a couple of minutes, her wet cheek pressed against mine. Then I released her gently and looked into her horror-stricken eyes.

"Now you've got to take some photographs," I said. "You're a Press photographer – that's your job."

She stared back at me, her eyes slowly becoming calmer. "I'll get your camera. I hope it's still all right." As I turned to fetch it I saw that a bullet had ripped a hole in the car door, just below the window.

The camera was unharmed. Miranda took it from me with shaking hands and I put the strap over her head, for fear that she would drop it. The muscles of her face tightened with determination as she began to adjust the focus.

By this time the Scots had rounded up the two English survivors and their sergeant was putting a field dressing on the wounded man's shoulder. A corporal examined the two who had fallen and satisfied himself that they were dead.

"Ask them the way to their headquarters, Bernie," I said.

Bernie put the question to the sergeant, who answered him without looking round. "He says they're in the fort – they've captured it. Shall we go there?"

"Yes," I replied. "It might make more sense than driving around looking for trouble." Bernie climbed into the driving seat and I opened the near side door.

"Wait a minute," said Miranda. "I haven't finished my job yet."

She crouched down and took a close-up shot of the dead Englishman, whose staring eyes were looking up at us in petrified astonishment. Then she turned and, without looking at me, climbed back into the car.

We drove off in silence, but after a few minutes I sensed a slight relaxation in the rigidity of Miranda's body, sitting beside me. She turned her head towards me and I was taken aback by the sparks of anger that I had never before seen in her eyes.

"I had to get that picture," she said. "Now I know what it's like, and I want other people to know, too. War, I mean. It's that boy, lying in the gutter, not knowing what's hit him, or why. They talk about freedom and rights, and all the stuff that Knox was going on about, but in the end it comes back to dead bodies and blood on the street. There has to be a better way of settling things."

Millions had said it before her, and many of them more eloquently; but she had just discovered it for herself, and the thought came from her lips with a fierce conviction that made me flinch. I felt a momentary sense of personal guilt at not having done something to prevent the tragedy we had just seen. It was irrational, but perhaps not completely, for I realized then that I hadn't felt the same sense of outrage as Miranda – and there had been a time when my reaction would have been the same as hers. Suddenly I saw her, not as an Aiseuropean, nor as a colleague, nor even as a beautiful woman, but as a person so like myself that in her company I might hope to be myself completely.

The sight of exultant Scotsmen swarming on the walls of the fort drove such philosophical reflections out of my mind. A jubilant Captain Mackie was at the gate to greet us.

CHAPTER 3

The fortnight that followed the capture of Newcastle was filled with frantic activity in both north and south. The Scots had taken some sixteen hundred prisoners – many literally in their beds – and had killed or wounded about two hundred of those who put up a brief resistance, suffering only trifling losses on their own side. Their booty had included four tanks, six armoured cars, twelve field-guns and a large quantity of small arms and ammunition. Although they were still markedly inferior, both in manpower and equipment, to their southern opponents, the military balance had been redressed a little in their favour.

The English, on the other hand, had been thrown into great confusion. On hearing of the Newcastle disaster the North English Regiment, instead of trying to take advantage of the vacuum in Scotland, immediately headed south by the western route, not pausing for breath till they got to Preston. The three and a half other regiments remaining intact were deployed (so Bernie learnt from a sergeant in the newly-formed Scottish Intelligence Corps) between Richmond and Hackney to guard against a surprise attack on London. And several officers were summarily relieved of their commands. (The Scots held a brigadier, two colonels and three majors among their prisoners).

I heard on the radio of acrimonious debates in the Assembly, but the government won every vote; and by the end of the first week Serjeant was talking confidently of a "short, sharp ending to this temporary interruption of the nation's progress". The main cause of his confidence may have been the supplies of sophisticated weaponry reportedly being flown in daily from Japan.

But arms had started coming into the north, too. On Newcastle station I watched the unloading of a train from Edinburgh and saw crates with Honanese labels, which were later broken open to reveal anti-tank rocket launchers. Rumour had it that concessions to drill for oil off the Scottish coast were being traded for arms; and I myself saw three Honanese whom I took to be businessmen arriving at the fort just as I was leaving after the daily briefing by Mackie (now a major).

Quite a sizeable Press Corps was growing up in Newcastle, which for the moment seemed to be functioning as the capital of Scotland, since Knox was spending most of his time there. Within the fortnight five television crews and about twenty journalists had arrived; and I had the unaccustomed experience of being treated with great respect because of my presence at the famous victory. I had even been interviewed twice on radio by the Japanese Broadcasting Corporation. There was also more than a trace of envy to be seen in my colleagues' eyes when they met me in the company of Miranda.

Mackie went to great lengths to keep us supplied with interesting information, most of it designed to show how rapidly Scotland was adjusting to its independent status – and how worthy of international recognition it was. There were a couple of conducted tours north of the Border, so that we could see things for ourselves; and a 'victory parade' was organized for the especial benefit of the television crews. Most of the participants in this display of military muscle – which included the captured armaments – were the recruits of four new regiments that had been raised and were being trained in the hills behind the town. (The actual victors of the battle had been carefully deployed by Johnston, now a Lieutenant-General, in positions farther to the south and west).

The parade was led by the Saint Andrew Armoured Regiment (named in imitation of the southern Saint George Regiment) with the captured tanks and armoured cars proudly painted with large, white, diagonal crosses. Then came token detachments from each of the four victorious battalions. These were followed by the new West Highland Regiment. While there was little uniformity in the appearance of the Highlanders, they all had blue and white brassards on their left arms and they were all wearing kilts. There were twenty or more tartans visible, each worn by a different formation. Some formations were around company strength while others numbered little more than a platoon.

Major Mackie explained that each clan had been allowed to form its own 'company', regardless of numbers. "It will be good for morale," he said. "And, of course, there are rivalries between some of the clans."

Each company seemed to have its own bagpiper, affrighting the air with a terrible wailing and screeching sound. I noticed that many of the Highlanders wore great swords, and altogether I thought them the wildest-looking bunch I had ever seen, with the possible exception of some Sumatran tribesmen who once gave me an uneasy half-hour.

By contrast, the Strathclyde Regiment seemed almost Japanese, dressed in captured British uniforms, with brassards. They were followed by the Eastern Highlanders, who looked very similar to the first formation – although I expect they wouldn't have thought so themselves. At the end of the column came the Border Rifles. Although they were dressed fairly uniformly in conventional battledress, their detachments also seemed to vary in size, and I questioned Mackie about this.

"Each of the great lords has formed a company from among his own tenants, like they used to in the old days," he told me. "They're very traditional in their ways, are the Border folk."

Knox himself, now adding the rank of General to his other titles, took the salute. When the parade was over he came and spoke to the journalists.

"Gentlemen," he declared, "you have been privileged to witness the beginning of a new era of peace in this island. Scotland has become a hedgehog with her own sharp prickles and will no longer seem such a tempting morsel to the hungry foxes of the south. The strength you have seen displayed today will never be used except in the defence of our sacred soil."

"General Knox, how soon do you intend to withdraw behind your own frontier again?" asked a television reporter from the Federated States.

Knox bared his teeth in a smile and shook a podgy finger at his questioner. "Now you're asking me to reveal a state secret, young man. All in good time. All in good time."

"Which country do you expect to be the first to recognize Scotland?" my fellow countryman from the *Rising Sun* asked.

"That's a very intelligent question," answered Knox, benevolently. "I would anticipate that before many days have passed the majority of peace-loving countries will have recognized our government. After all," he smiled knowingly, "Scotland has a great deal to offer those who are her friends."

"When will the date for elections to the Constituent Assembly be announced?" I enquired.

Knox turned and beamed at me, radiating good will. "Mr. Hashimoto – with us from the beginning and still here to see the second chapter unfold," he said. "The Assembly elections will be held the very moment that peace is assured. I am eager to lay down some of the heavy burdens that have fallen on me, and to have around me the support of those who will voice the wisdom of the people."

When the impromptu Press conference was over we walked back to the Kyoto Hotel. "There's talk that Knox is asking for a new frontier along the Roman Wall," remarked Bernie.

"Oh! I hadn't heard that one," I said. "It's probably a bargaining position, on the basis that you should always ask for more than what you expect to get."

The bells began to clang in the tower of the Christian temple beside the fort. It was an air raid warning. We had had several attacks by the British Air Force in the past week. Single Typhoon fighters had flown low across the town and dropped small bombs around the railway lines on the north side, without doing any damage. Once the bombs had fallen in the river, near the docks. Whether the pilots were afraid to aim at any target which could involve the risk of hitting their compatriots still living in the town, or whether some other policy lay behind their tactics, I couldn't tell.

We saw the plane almost at once – a rapidly expanding black dot in the southern sky. "He's just too late for the parade," said Bernie.

In a moment it was over us, and we saw the rockets leave its underside with great spurts of white smoke that trailed behind them as they streaked towards the south wall of the fort, exploding in four blinding yellow flashes. Thick black smoke billowed into the sky, and the plane had gone. We ran back the three or four hundred metres to the edge of the ditch surrounding the fort, scarcely noticing the fragments of masonry that littered the roadway under our feet. There were four ragged gaps, somewhat smaller than I had expected, in the wall above us, revealing shattered rooms behind.

"His aim was a bit better that time," said Bernie. Miranda was busy with her camera. We hung around for a while and eventually heard that one soldier had been killed and two injured in the attack.

The bells rang again just as we were about to enter the hotel, and a minute later there was a multiple explosion like the first. Once again the black smoke billowed up from the direction of the fort. This time we ran to the car, which was parked nearby, and drove back the way we had come.

"Knox has just discovered the place where his hedgehog has no prickles," I said. "He's completely without air defences."

"But there can't be many air forces smaller than ours," said Miranda.

"I know there are only three of those Typhoons," I replied, "but they can keep flying them all day and all night if they want to. And even the little trainers could be used for dropping bombs. I'm surprised they haven't done more with their planes before now. But unless Knox's Honanese friends can help him with this one he'll have to get his head down and try a different kind of warfare altogether."

"What could they give him?" Miranda asked. "Planes?"

"They might, but it would be pretty difficult, I think, at least until they'd decided to recognize him. But they have a pretty effective ground-to-air missile – though they'd have to send the men to use it, as well."

"And then Serjeant will have to get somebody else – Japanese, I suppose – to come and show him what to do about it. It'll be just like the old days," said Bernie, bringing the car to a halt in the square in front of the fort.

This time there was no sign of damage to the outer walls, but smoke was drifting up sluggishly from the interior of the great black fortress. The sentries on the main gate could tell us nothing, except that the rockets had exploded inside. However, it soon became clear that an evacuation was beginning. Four armoured cars drove out, one of them heavily scratched and dented, followed by a steady stream of trucks and cars.

Two of the trucks parked in front of the nearby temple and soldiers started unloading bedding and carrying it inside. I recognized the sergeant in charge as the one whose bullets had so narrowly missed us in the shooting incident, and went over to talk to him. Eight men had been killed and seventeen wounded, and three trucks had been destroyed, he said. He was angry and frustrated at not being able to hit back at the aircraft. As I returned to the car I glance up at the battlements and caught sight of Knox and Mackie looking down.

We were having our evening meal at the hotel when the windows rattled at the impact of yet another explosion. "Funny," said Bernie, "I didn't hear a plane this time."

"Maybe there's been an accident," I said.

A few minutes later a page-boy came to tell me that I was wanted on the telephone. It was Major Mackie.

"No doubt you heard the explosion," he said. "I thought you and your colleagues would want to know that it was a delayed action bomb which must have been dropped by one of the two enemy aircraft this afternoon. Most regrettably there are a number of civilian casualties – English civilians. If your colleagues should want to take pictures, let them know that we will be very willing to supply arc lights."

The majority of the other journalists and the television crews were staying at the Kyoto, and we all went down together to the scene of the tragedy. Earlier in the day I had noticed the two single-storied stone cottages built on the edge of the dry moat. I had noticed them because of a girl standing beside them, looking up with frightened eyes at the smoking gaps in the fortress wall, a small child clutching at her skirt and crying. She had long, black hair and her blouse was partly unbuttoned, revealing two beautifully-rounded white breasts. Now there was only a pile of smoking ruins where the cottages had been.

Mackie was there to greet us, his face drawn and serious; and already the arc lights were being put in position. The television cameras would need them in the failing evening light.

"We've found a fragment of the bomb," he announced. "A sentry thought he saw something fall on the edge of the moat during the second raid today, but when a couple of my men had a look later they couldn't find anything – most unfortunately."

He showed us a twisted piece of tail-fin. "Just like the one that fell over by the railway," Bernie remarked. "Same yellow marking at the top."

Mackie overhead him. "Yes. It's exactly the same," he confirmed. "There's no doubt about it."

He wasn't certain of the exact number of casualties because nobody seemed to know how many of the inhabitants had been out of their homes when the bomb went off. But so far five bodies had been uncovered, three of them children, and two badly injured women had been taken to the hospital. Men from neighbouring houses were helping the soldiers dig among the ruins, and as we turned to watch a shout went up from one gang. They had found somebody else.

I watched as three kilted soldiers and two young civilians tugged at a thick, splintered beam and pulled it out of the pile of masonry. One of the soldiers stooped down into the cavity and lifted out the body of a woman. It was twisted and shapeless, like a scarecrow at the end of summer, but I saw the long, black hair that trailed from the head, thick and lustrous under a powdering of dust, and I guessed that it must be the girl I had seen earlier.

I turned, away feeling sick. Miranda, who had taken several photographs, was retching. I put my arm around her shoulders and led her away. Bernie had disappeared, but we went and sat in the car. Then Miranda laid her head on my shoulder in such a trusting, child-like way that for the moment the only emotion I could feel towards her was a paternal tenderness.

We sat in silence for several minutes and then she said, "I'm sorry. I don't seem to be much good at the war bit. Maybe it's not a woman's job, after all."

"Being a woman hasn't all that much to do with it," I said. "A man the same age as you, who had the same amount of experience, would probably have reacted in much the same way. He might have covered it up a bit more, but his photographs wouldn't have been any better. And if he was so insensitive that he didn't get upset, then he'd never make a good news photographer. He'd be nothing but a holiday snapshot man."

She gave a little snorting laugh and lifted her head. "Thanks," she said, looking at me with that warm glow radiating again from her eyes. My feelings were no longer paternal.

"I wonder where Bernie has got to," she said. "He just seemed to disappear."

"I don't know – perhaps we'd better go and look for him. Feeling all right now?" She nodded.

We were getting out of the car when Bernie reappeared, walking slowly towards us, and we went to meet him. Miranda slipped her arm through mine, and I felt my stomach muscles contract with excitement.

"I've just heard something very peculiar," said Bernie when we came up to him. "About this business." He jerked his thumb over his shoulder towards the scene of the disaster.

"What about it?" I enquired.

"I've been talking to a little lad – about eleven or twelve – who says he lives down the street and used to play with the boy in the first cottage. He says about five minutes before the explosion he saw two Scotty soldiers carrying a big box round behind the cottages."

"Probably some detector equipment," I said. "Remember? Mackie said they'd already looked for an unexploded bomb."

Bernie shook his head. "But the boy says that when they came back again they didn't have it with them. They'd left it there. He was going to go and look at it, he says, but his mother called him to go home."

"You mean it wasn't an unexploded bomb at all," said Miranda. "It was planted there by… by Mackie or somebody? But why would they want to do a thing like that?"

"I can think of one good reason," I said, slowly. "When the news gets out that the English hit their own people by mistake there'll be a lot of pressure to stop using the planes, at least against targets in built-up areas. And then if the Scots stick close to English houses they won't need any anti-aircraft defences. I thought it was a bit odd that Mackie was on the scene so quickly with his arc lights, and everything."

"That bit of tail-fin wasn't *like* the one they found by the railway," said Bernie. "It *was* the one. I knew I'd seen it before."

"But that's disgusting," Miranda said, looking towards the pool of light where the rescuers were still digging. "It's worse than disgusting."

"It's war," I said. "Let's go and find anybody else who saw anything. I haven't got very much to go on, if this story's going to be believed."

We walked back and mingled with the watching crowd, but could discover no one else who had been around before the explosion, nor was there any sign of the boy, who had run away when Bernie had asked him to come and repeat his story to me. Mackie saw us talking to people and came across.

"Just trying to get some background on the victims," I said. "It would add human interest to the story."

"Yes, indeed," he nodded. "Incidentally, I've just heard that General Knox is giving a personal donation to assist the survivors. You might like to tell your readers that."

Miranda turned her back and walked rapidly away. And then I remembered seeing Knox and Mackie on the battlements, looking down – it must have been at those two cottages. "That's very interesting," I said. "I must make a note of it."

When we were back at the car I said, "This is one story that I can't see Mackie allowing to get on to the wire – not the way I'm going to write it. Later on, when things are quiet, I think we ought to start heading south."

And so we later set out through the night, trying not to attract attention. On the far side of the river a patrol stopped us, but when we explained that we were on our way to visit the front line headquarters in Darlington (forward defences had now been established on the line of the River Tees) they allowed us to proceed.

We were careful to avoid Darlington, crossing the Tees much higher up, at a village called Barnard Castle, and then travelling southward on a road which – so Miranda said – skirted the edge of the beautiful Yorkshire Dales. However, we could see nothing but the road ahead of us, white in the glare of the headlights.

We entered a small town in which the great black shape of a temple suddenly loomed up in the starlight above the shadowy houses, and Miranda said, "We're in Ripon. It won't be long now before we get to York." I had heard that York was held by the North English Regiment, who had moved across from Preston. And since it was the provincial capital I expected to be able to send off my story from there.

Just before Barnard Castle Bernie had begun to be worried about the nearside front tyre. It felt like a slow puncture, he said. Probably we'd picked up a splinter in the square after the explosion. Sure enough, the tyre was soft when we checked it, but an application of the foot-pump made it firm again. We had had to use the pump again about three-quarters of an hour later; and now, when we had left Ripon some ten kilometres behind us, there was a shuddering sensation, and Bernie quickly applied the brakes. "I'll have to change that wheel," he said. "There's a spare in the back."

It was a slow business, changing the wheel by the light of the small emergency lamp, but at length we succeeded. The first light of morning was streaking the sky as we climbed back into the car. I was about to shut the door when Miranda raised her hand and exclaimed, "Ssh! What's that noise?" I listened, and heard a faint thumping sound, far to the south.

"Gunfire," I said, "almost certainly. Something pretty heavy."

"Maybe it's Johnston, trying another of his dawn attacks," said Bernie, starting the engine. "I wonder if it'll work as well as the first one."

"He might be having a go at the airfield at York," I said. "The Typhoons were supposed to be operating from there."

The sounds of battle grew louder as we travelled to the south-east, but after about half-an-hour they stopped. We could see now that we had reached the outskirts of York, and Bernie drove cautiously. To the left, and perhaps two kilometres ahead of us, a column of black smoke swirled up into the sky.

The road wound through a hamlet of low, stone cottages, and I noticed as we passed the first of these that their doors were open. One door was swinging to and fro in the morning breeze. Rounding the bend, we almost ran into three soldiers. They were kilted Highlanders, and their arms were full of plunder they must have taken from the cottages. I saw women's dresses, a dead chicken, cheeses, a sewing-machine and several pairs of shoes.

As Bernie braked hard the three swung round to face us. Two were dark, with bristling beards, and one of these had a bloodstained bandage on his left forearm. The third was very tall, with red hair, a white skin and a straggling red moustache. The redhead dropped his loot and unslung the rifle from his shoulder in one swift movement. He aimed at our windscreen and shouted. Bernie wound down the window and spoke to him in English, but the Highlander kept on shouting and his words didn't sound like English to me.

“Can’t make out what this fellow’s saying,” said Bernie, his face puckered with anxiety. “He’s talking in Gaelic. But I think he wants us to get out – and I don’t like the way he’s handling that gun. See what I mean?”

I saw what he meant, and we got out of the car without further delay. Redhead got into the driving seat and started examining the vehicle, stroking the upholstery and turning the controls on the dashboard. It was evident from his movements that he hadn’t had much close contact with cars before, and probably knew nothing about how they worked.

The other two seemed more interested in Miranda. They stared at her fixedly with their dark, blue eyes. When she drew her long black cloak more tightly around her the one with the blood-stained bandage put out his hand and tried to pull it aside. Miranda shrank away from him, and at the same moment I instinctively stepped forward. His companion thrust the muzzle of his rifle towards me, menacingly, and I stood still. The man with the bandage followed Miranda and grabbed the cloak near the collar. I saw her mouth open, but no sound came out from between her lips. He pulled the cloak downward and she let it go, so that it fell to the ground.

Miranda was wearing a white sweater, very Eastern in cut, which moulded itself to the lovely lines of her body. The two men exclaimed together – in admiration, so it sounded. She spoke to them, huskily, in English, but they shook their heads. Then the one with the bandage said something to his companion and they both laughed. Their laughter had a savage ring to it. She was standing near the front of the car, and suddenly the man with the bandage seized her by the shoulders and threw her backwards, so that she lay across the bonnet. Miranda screamed – a single despairing scream.

I knew as I moved that it was going to be futile, but my legs instinctively carried me forward. The soldier with the rifle was no longer watching me, having transferred his attention again to Miranda. I aimed a kick in the direction of his crotch, realizing too late that the leather pouch suspended from his belt wasn’t worn in that position entirely for ornament. My toe caught it squarely, but the impact must have been cushioned, for he merely grunted and took a step backward.

Redhead had just got out of the car, and from the corner of my eye I saw him level his rifle at my head. They say that in the instant before death all kinds of philosophical thoughts or concentrated flashes of memory pass through the mind. All I can remember thinking then was, "What a squalid, futile way to finish."

I heard a click, but there was no blinding flash or searing pain. The Highlander had already emptied his magazine. But he instantly raised the weapon above his head like a club and rushed at me. The rifle swung down in a wide arc towards my head. I ducked and the barrel struck me on the left shoulder, spinning me round. My knees buckled and I fell to the ground.

When I hit the roadway I let my head fall back, mouth open, and lay quite still, hoping that the Highlander would think he had stunned me. Apparently he did, for when I cautiously opened my eyes a minute later he had turned and was thrusting himself between his two companions.

For a moment I thought he was trying to prevent them from molesting Miranda, but then I realized that he was merely asserting the privilege of superior rank, or strength.

Miranda kicked out at him and her booted left foot caught him on the chest. He staggered back and growled in fury, striking her across the face with his huge red hand. She cried out in pain, but seemed to recover quickly and tried to slide down from the bonnet. The other two grabbed her and she struggled furiously to escape them, but to no effect. They hoisted her up and held her by the shoulders, face down this time, across the bonnet.

Redhead thrust his fingers under the tight waistband of her black skirt and tugged, but at first it didn't yield. Then there was a tearing sound and he dragged the skirt off and threw it on the ground. Miranda was wearing brief white knickers under a pair of black tights. The three men shouted hoarsely, again in admiration, by the sound of it. They seemed to be exchanging jokes as the red-haired one dragged the tights down and left them hanging around her ankles. She kicked out again, but he stepped aside to avoid her feet and took hold of the elasticated top of her knickers.

I looked around in desperation. Bernie seemed to have disappeared. I couldn't blame him – there wasn't much point in getting himself killed in a hopeless struggle. But I knew that I had to make one last attempt, and it almost certainly would be the last. With my head I didn't subscribe to a single one of those romantic notions of what manly virtue required me to do; but I knew they were too deeply imbedded in my emotions to let me live with myself if I didn't try.

The only realistic hope was that I might create a diversion for long enough to let Miranda break free and run away. Maybe terror would lend her legs enough speed. Then I saw a rifle lying on the ground a couple of metres from me. If I could reach it, and if my numb left arm would allow me to raise it, there might yet be a chance.

The redheaded soldier had pulled the knickers below her knees and was sinking the fingers of his great, red hands into the naked flesh of her buttocks. I knew that if I was inside that man's skin it would take nothing less, now, than a bullet through the head to stop me from finishing what I had begun. I raised myself on my right elbow and prepared to make a dive for the rifle, wondering whether I'd be able to fire it, since I'd never handled one of those Ch'i automatics before.

The man with the bandaged arm must have seen my movement, for he shouted and let go of Miranda, grabbing for his weapon, which was leaning against the car. At the same moment there was a great bellow from down the road in front of us. Two figures came running round the bend. In front was Bernie, very red in the face, and a couple of paces behind him a white-bearded Highlander with a magnificent feather, half a metre high, in the side of his bonnet.

The newcomer, an officer I guessed, shouted to the soldiers in Gaelic. They stood irresolute, two of them still holding Miranda and the third with his hand on the barrel of his rifle. Then the red-haired one shouted an answer and, letting go of Miranda's bottom, began to hitch up the front of his kilt. His reply seemed to enrage the running officer, who shook his fist and ran harder.

Redhead hesitated, his kilt held up in both hands, and shouted again, in a querulous, pleading tone this time. But the white-bearded officer had now come up to the group, and as he drew level with them he unsheathed a great sword with a basket hilt that was swinging by his side. With the flat of its blade he struck the red-haired soldier a resounding blow across the shoulders. The man staggered forward, and then ducked and ran to avoid a second blow. The officer next turned his attention to the soldier who was holding Miranda, catching him on the right arm with the flat of the blade. As he swung the gleaming weapon he shouted furiously, and his face was as scarlet as the setting sun. The three Highlanders waited for no more chastisement, but picked up their rifles and took to their heels in the direction from which the officer had come.

Miranda slid to the ground as Bernie and I ran towards her, and her knees seemed to buckle under her. Bernie helped her to stand, while I picked up her cloak and put it around her shoulders. The white-bearded officer confronted us, sword in hand. He removed his bonnet with a flourish, bowing low to Miranda and addressing her in English. I assumed that he was making an apology. She murmured something faintly in reply.

Then he spoke to me in Japanese, pronouncing his words carefully, with a slightly musical inflection, "I very much regret that men of my clan should have behaved so wickedly, but you will understand that they have not been under military discipline for very long. The excitement of the battle must have made them forgetful of who they were. I trust they have not done you any injury."

I was all right, I said. (Sensation was now coming back into my left arm, though I guessed there would be some pretty bruises on my shoulder.)

"Will you be returning to the north with us?" he asked. "I shall be happy to provide you with an escort."

"Aren't you going to stay in York, then?" I enquired.

"No – we've just been showing the Sassenachs that Scotland has a long arm. And we caught one of their aeroplanes on the ground and blew it sky-high." He laughed, and his white-bearded face now looked jolly, like a benevolent old gentleman.

"I think we'll go to the south," I said. "I'd like to see what effect this has had on the English morale." (It seemed like a reason the Scotsman might find acceptable.)

He laughed again. "They'll be running around like a lot of..." He searched his memory for the Japanese word. "... a lot of rabbits. Well, if that's the way you're going let me wish you a safe journey. I'll give you a little piece of paper to help you, should you meet any more of our men."

He sheathed his sword, replaced his bonnet on his head, and took a piece of paper from his pouch. On it he laboriously wrote a few words, and handed it to me, saying with a chuckle, "Don't show it to the English – if you ever catch up with them." Then he bowed again to Miranda, and strode away.

I picked up her skirt from where the Highlander had thrown it, and brought it to her. I couldn't think what I should say to comfort her. She turned her back and began to pull up her tights, underneath the cloak. I saw that the waistband of the skirt was torn, so I took off my necktie and offered it to her, saying, "You can use this as a belt, to hold it up." She took it from me, nodding dumbly.

"Bernie," I said, "let's get away from this place."

He went around to the driving seat and I opened the door for Miranda. As she started to climb in I put my hand on her waist, to help her. She looked at me, her face drawn and expressionless and her eyes half-closed, and said, "Don't touch me – please."

Bernie started the engine and we drove to the south. As the car moved into green countryside, unmarked by any trace of battle, I began to relax. My shoulder throbbed, but I felt the light-headed euphoria that comes from a realization that one's head has been inside the jaws of death and out again before they had time to close on it. And beside me sat a beautiful woman who had just seen me twice risk my life to protect her honour. It was the kind of romantic situation that even a war correspondent couldn't expect to come his way more than once in a lifetime.

I must be very gentle now with Miranda, I thought, because of the shock she had suffered. But before very long she would surely repay the debt of gratitude she must be feeling towards me.

Laying my hand lightly on her knee, I asked, "How are you feeling now?"

She jerked her leg away violently, jogging Bernie's arm so that he made the car swerve right across the road. "Don't touch me! I don't ever want anyone to touch me again," she exclaimed in a hoarse voice that struggled with an unfamiliar emotion.

"I wouldn't hurt you, Miranda. You know that," I said, soothingly. "It's all over now. You've got to relax and try to forget."

"No. You wouldn't do it the way they tried to," she replied, "but you want to, all the same. You want to take my body and degrade me. You're all the same. But I won't let you. I won't let anyone touch me." Her voice rose in a note of hysteria, and I was so taken by surprise I could think of nothing to say.

"Why don't you put your head back and try to get some sleep. You must be worn out," said Bernie, very casually, sounding as if he hadn't been listening.

It was half-an-hour before Miranda nodded into a fitful sleep, but she didn't speak again. I sat tensely beside her, trying to avoid any accidental contact across the few centimetres that separated us. The euphoria had gone and in its place the numbness of deepening disappointment matched the physical ache that pervaded my shoulder.

CHAPTER 4

Hot sunshine was streaming down from the blue Mediterranean sky as the Air Europa Unitas 217 taxied across Marseille airport for take-off. I wondered if the sun would also be shining in London when we arrived. I had never seen Britain in really fine weather, and by this time its summer would be over.

After the raid on York there had been a lull in the fighting in Britain, with both sides recruiting, training and borrowing to build up their new armies. And since this had coincided with an outbreak of civil war in the Tyrrhenian Union, my paper had transferred me to cover the new story. (Incidentally, my "sensational disclosure" about the origin of the Newcastle explosion never got published. The Foreign Editor told me later that he'd spiked it because the evidence wasn't strong enough and publication might have implied a bias against the Scots.) And I soon became aware that the *Nagoya Guardian* was strongly opposed to the Japanese Prime Minister's support for the British government.

I had been reluctant to leave Britain, partly because I felt very much involved in the war but more because of Miranda. She had never again spoken about the incident with the Highlanders, but it lay between us like a land-mine. Her attitude towards me had changed from openness and trust to guarded reserve, and in the fortnight I was with her after our return to the south I never once heard her laugh. Her relationship with Bernie seemed to have altered less, and I even felt jealous – an emotion I thought I was immune to – when she occasionally smiled at him. The high hopes I had had of physical as well as mental intimacy were gone, and yet I found myself wanting it more than ever before. Then I had had to leave, not knowing whether I would ever see her again, and not even the Mediterranean sun could dispel the chill that my spirits took from her frigidly polite farewell.

The new story had several similarities to the British situation but a lot of differences as well. The people in the northern part of the straggling Tyrrhenian Union, itself a Muslim segment carved out of the predominantly Christian European Empire at the time of Independence, felt themselves oppressed by the majority to the south, and finally exploded in open revolt. It was the Union's northern provinces – Savoy, Grenoble, Provence and Liguria – that rebelled against the islanders of Corsica, Sardinia and Sicily and the Africans of Tunisia and Libya, among all of whom Arab blood was much more dominant. Unlike the Scots, they had no distinctive units of their own in the armed forces, and the opening stages of the revolt were characterized more by massacre and repression than by armed resistance. The gutters of Marseille, Grenoble and Genoa ran with the blood of butchered students, professors and civil servants.

Then Europa decided to intervene, and it was only a matter of days before the Tyrrhenian government forces had been rounded up or swept into the sea. I entered the rebel provinces in the wake of a European armoured division which swept down the Rhone Valley, meeting and crushing some fierce resistance near Montelimar.

The retreating government soldiers burned, looted and blew up a swathe of devastation, and for several weeks after the fighting had ended only a massive foreign relief operation kept much of the country fed. I accompanied a Swiss battalion (the Swiss, although they have always maintained independence in their land-locked, mountainous country, still supply soldiers to the European Army, just as they did under the Japanese Empire) in pursuit of a Sicilian battalion that tried to take refuge in the Maritime Alps, and for the first time in my life I saw people actually dying of hunger. However, only the very old and some of the young children were at the point of death, and most of them were saved when a helicopter brought in food the following day. But I shall never forget the sight of a tall, fair-haired Swiss rifleman gently unclasping the tightly clinging arms of a mother from around the pot-bellied, matchstick-limbed body of her dead child. The black veil had slipped down from her shrunken cheeks, and her large, brown eyes were filled with an uncomprehending despair.

I wondered what horrors might be in store for the British, now that their war seemed to be moving into a new phase. By all accounts, both sides had finally acquired enough hardware to be able to do each other some real damage – although the balance was probably even more heavily weighted in favour of the London government than it had been at the beginning. They enjoyed the advantages of legitimacy – no one had yet recognized Knox's regime – and they had been able to impose at least a partial blockade on the rebels.

My reflections were interrupted by the man sitting next to me, a tall, middle-aged Japanese whom I had seen at the previous day's Presidential press conference. "I sometimes wonder if these pinkies don't occasionally regret the day when they kissed the Empire good-bye," he remarked. "I don't mean the politicians – they've been having a ball ever since we left – but the poor buggers who have to watch their houses bombed and their crops destroyed in all these little wars. Whatever else we did, at least we gave them a bit of peace and order."

"Yes, I suppose we did," I replied, "once we'd finished conquering them. But over the last sixty years East Asia hasn't exactly been a haven of peace and tranquillity. This business was a tea ceremony compared with our last war."

A young man sitting in the third seat in our row, by the window, joined in the conversation. "Don't you think that the resort to violent self-assertion is an essential ingredient in the process of seeking national identity?" he asked. Although he looked Japanese his accent marked him unmistakably as a citizen of the Federated States. "In my opinion the denial of an opportunity to engage in an armed liberation struggle was the final disservice inflicted by Japanese imperialism on its colonial victims."

I heard my neighbour utter a long, low hissing sound between his teeth. "You mean you think we ought to have had a fight with the buggers instead of giving them their independence peaceably?" he asked incredulously.

"Well, I wouldn't express it in exactly that way," replied the young man, "but it seems to me that the lack of a cohesive multicultural infrastructure, which is the post-colonial characteristic of ex-Japanese territories, in contradistinction to what may be observed in such former Honanese colonies as Borneo – and Greece, of course – points to a hiatus in psycho-sociological development. The missing catalytic ingredient would appear to be experience of revolutionary violence in the self-achievement process of national liberation. By denying this fundamental human right, it seems to me, Japanese imperialism perpetrated – maybe at a sub-conscious level of awareness – a psycho-dynamic prolongation of the quintessential dominance-subservience relationship. A structured analysis of the ethno-political disorientation of a hetero-societal agglomeration such as Europa leads one inescapably to that conclusion."

"Does it indeed?" said the tall journalist (who, I later discovered, worked for Affiliated Press), elevating his eyebrows until they seemed about to touch his hairline. "I take it you're not on a media assignment?"

"No," said the young man. "I'm working on a doctoral thesis. I'm here on a travel fellowship – just at the right moment, it seems."

"What's the subject of your thesis?" I asked.

"Violence as a catalytic factor in the achievement of meaningful national self-identification," he replied.

"Does that mean you think violence is a good thing?" asked the AP man.

"That's a generalization to which I couldn't assent without reservation," the student replied. "For example, within the framework of an established proletarian autarcho-democracy counter-revolutionary violence would clearly be productive of retrogressive socio-economic trends, although the peace-oriented violence employed to negative its disruptive potentialities could have a beneficial end-product in the revival of dormant centrifugal loyalty-orientation."

"I see," said the AP man. "And what about this war in Britain? Do you think it will have a good effect on their loyalty-orientations?"

The student knitted his brows in concentration. "That's a hypothesis that I haven't fully considered yet," he said. "I'm hoping to make an appraisal of the existential dynamics of the situation at first hand – providing the limitations on linguistic comprehension don't create an insuperable block to feedback in the communication process."

"You don't speak English, then?" I asked.

"That's right," he replied. "But I don't anticipate a major problem, since there are certain readily ascertainable indicators by which the existence of a pre-revolutionary situation can be authenticated."

"Britain's not exactly pre-revolutionary," said the AP man. "They had their revolution six months ago."

The student corrected him. "That wasn't a true revolution. It was an assertion of ethnic sub-group identity, articulated by reactionary social elements in a temporary leadership stance. I'm hopeful, however, that the concomitant violence may escalate to the requisite intensity for a socio-economic confrontation between the exploitive and exploited classes to be generated."

"You mean you hope that a lot of people will be killed and there'll be a complete breakdown in law and order?" asked the AP man.

"What you call law and order is simply one of the mechanisms of exploitation," retorted the student. "And of course a somewhat elevated curve of fatalities is to be anticipated in the climactic phase of the liberation struggle. Although it is to be regretted in terms of the consequent dislocation of the social micro-units involved, it has to be accepted as part of the price of achieving autarcho-democratic viability."

"What do you mean by a social micro-unit?" I enquired.

He looked surprised. "Why, a kinship group, of course," he said. "You know – a family. That kind of thing."

"So you think that when they've smashed up what little they've got, and there's a raging famine, they'll push over their elected Assembly and set up an 'autarcho-democratic' system?" asked the AP man.

"Total socio-economic collapse might not be a prerequisite," the student replied, "but from the inconclusive scenario which we have witnessed here in Provence, I'm afraid that it will be – though of course, it might be forestalled in a similar way in Britain, by the intervention of neo-imperialist elements in the guise of humanitarian assistance."

"How do you mean?" I asked.

"Well, if it had not been for the importation of large quantities of foodstuffs by international agencies enmeshed in the power structures of the neo-imperialist states – and by some of their pseudo-autarcho-democratic collaborationists – the inadequacies of the non-participatory infrastructure being created by the quasi-revolutionary regime would have been exposed, and the proletariat would have had an incentive to reject that infrastructure before it became entrenched. As it is, the neo-imperialists have already established a relationship of dependence, while simultaneously reinforcing at a subliminal level in the collective subconscious an illusion of their own omnicompetence.

And so the posture of their puppet regime has been rendered less susceptible to challenge."

"You'd be in favour of letting a few more of the buggers starve, so that the rest of them would start the Revolution Mark Two?" asked the AP man.

"If they don't starve now they'll probably starve at a future date, when the incompetence of their government activates a situation of economic malfunction. Sentimentality has no role to perform in the scientific analysis of the historical process," said the student.

"Tell me," said the AP man, "what do you plan to do with this thesis of yours, when you've written it."

The student smiled modestly and replied, "Well, there's a publisher in New Toyama who has expressed a moderate degree of interest."

"And I suppose he'll pay you good money for it?"

"A realistic pecuniary arrangement would be an integral part of any contractual agreement," replied the student, nodding seriously. We had now taken off, and the AP man lit a cigarette, inhaled deeply and blew a long, thin jet of smoke over the top of the seat in front. It's occupant coughed violently. Then there was a long silence.

"If you two will pardon me," said the student eventually, "I've got some notes I'd like to transcribe from my recorder. I want to clear the tape before we get to Britain." He produced a miniature tape recorder, fitted the ear-piece into his ear and began to write in a notebook.

About half an hour later the AP man, who had just awakened from a short nap, remarked to me in a low voice, "You know I've often wondered – though I'm sure our friend here would think me a reactionary neo-imperialist for saying so – whether these pinkies are really capable of getting out of the mess they're in. I doubt if we could do it, in the same situation. The millions of kids you see down there, all over the place," he pointed his finger at the floor of the plane, "what are they going to do when they grow up? There's not nearly enough land to go round and they don't have the industries in the towns to cope with them."

"They've got a lot of resources that haven't been developed yet," I said.

"A certain amount," he conceded. "But the point is, will they ever be able to develop them on their own? I can understand them not wanting to have us doing it any longer, and taking the lion's share of the profits – I'm not as reactionary as our friend might think. But they just don't seem to have the aptitude for it. I'm not saying that's entirely a bad thing. They may know more about how to enjoy life than we do. But you must admit it's a bit of a handicap in this day and age, with the kind of problems they've got to cope with."

"Maybe they've never had the chance to discover their aptitudes," I said. "After all, we didn't exactly encourage a spirit of enterprise when we were in charge."

"That's not the point," he replied. "We'd already developed our resources when we got here. But we both had the same opportunities at the beginning. The fact remains, it was a Taiwanese ship that sailed into Oporto, and not a Portuguese ship that reached Kaohsiung."

I nodded. "It's difficult to think what the world would be like if things had been the other way round."

"It's impossible," said the AP man. "I'm no historian, but it seems pretty plain to me there was no other way it could have happened. Things developed the way they did because of the patterns that were already laid down when civilizations were starting. I know the Europeans had their ancient Roman Empire and it reached quite a high level. Some interesting remains of it back there at a place called Avignon." He jerked his thumb over his shoulder, to indicate the direction from which we had come. "Maybe if that Empire hadn't broken up they'd have gone on developing, but the point is, it did."

"I'm no expert on Occidental history, either," I said, "but I think they got going again quite well after that – just like East Asia did after the break-up of the Tang Empire. Even in Britain I saw some quite impressive temples dating back about seven or eight hundred years. But just think – supposing the Mongols hadn't overrun a large part of Europa. Supposing they'd turned their horses' heads in the opposite direction and come right down into East Asia instead. Don't you think that might have made a lot of difference to what happened later?"

He shook his head. "The Mongols were only here for about a hundred years. We've had interruptions in our history, too."

"But if the Mongol occupation hadn't weakened them they might have been able to resist the Turks. That was what really killed their chances of developing their own civilization."

"If it hadn't been one thing it would have been another," the AP man replied. "For all those centuries they had the empty lands quite close to them across the Atlantic – much closer than they were to us. They had coal and iron underneath the ground. In all probability they've got more than us, but they only scratched at it till we came. And they had a good mixture of nations and languages – plenty of competition – just like we had in East Asia. There just seems to be something missing. Maybe it's their religion, making them fatalistic. You know, they believe their god decides what's going to happen and there's not much they can do about it – except try to keep in with him."

"I still think a lot more has happened because of accidents than because of anything to do with the kinds of people that we are," said I. "Two thousand years ago these Westerners had their Roman Empire and East Asia had the Han. They both disappeared; and in another two thousand years the centres of power may be somewhere completely different from where they are today – or we may all have blown ourselves up."

He nodded glumly. "One thing's certain – you and I won't be here to see it."

The student, who had fallen asleep with his ear-piece still in position, stirred and opened his eyes. He retrieved his fallen notebook and switched on the recorder again. I wondered what new data he would accumulate in Britain.

When we landed at London Airport it was raining. No wonder Aizawa Shoin called Britain 'The Grey Island' when he first discovered it.

The customs and immigration checks were much more thorough this time than on my first visit, and I noticed soldiers armed with sub-machine-guns stationed at strategic points. On entering the Arrivals Lounge I immediately saw the round, red face of Bernie, grinning in welcome, and hovering over him the tall, slim figure of Marlowe, the *Guardian*'s stringer in Britain. No Miranda. I felt like a man who returns from work on a winter evening expecting a hot meal to be waiting for him, and finds his home dark and deserted.

Bernie had the Rough Rider in the car park and we set out immediately for London. "I thought when you heard the latest news you'd want to start for the north as soon as possible," said Marlowe.

"What's been happening, then?" I asked.

"The Big Push has begun this morning," Marlowe told me. "It seems that the government forces are advancing on two fronts. They've got pretty well complete control of the air, though I've heard that one Typhoon has been shot down by anti-aircraft fire. The Scots claim to have destroyed seven, but the Air Force doesn't have more than six. There's been heavy fighting around Darlington, and a sea-borne attack on Hartlepool. That's about everything I've heard, so far. Have you heard anything else, Bernie?"

"Only that the Scots have laid a lot of mines, and some of the tanks have taken a pasting on them," said Bernie.

"Do you think Knox will be able to hold out for long?" I asked Marlowe.

"Not if the government can keep up the pressure," he replied. "Of course, Johnston's a clever general – he's shown that several times. But the Scots just don't have the fire-power, in spite of all the stuff the Honanese have been giving them."

"Why are the Honanese so anxious to help? Do they seriously think Knox will keep control of the oil and give them the concession?"

Marlowe nodded. "That's what it looks like. You know as well as I do that oil is fast becoming liquid gold. And that could also have something to do with why the Japanese government has been so vigorous in its aid to Serjeant. We could never have afforded all the equipment that's been pouring in if we weren't buying now and promising to pay later. Of course, Serjeant has much the stronger hand to play, with a lot of other mineral prospecting rights beginning to look interesting. For instance, a Federated States company has just finished a survey in South Wales and says there are huge coal reserves there – quite close to the sea. If Serjeant can ride out this storm he could be in calm waters for a long time to come."

"Well," I said, "it looks as if I'm in time to see the crisis in the fever. Either the patient will die or he'll start to recover. How soon can we get to the north, Bernie?"

“Have you up there by tonight, captain,” Bernie replied. “You’d better stop in York and have a bit of shut-eye, after all the travelling you’ve been doing. And we can pick up Miranda there in the morning. She said she’d be ready.”

I had been a stranger to hope for so long that just for a moment I was bewildered by its return, and I wondered why the rain had suddenly become soft and welcoming. It was good to be back in Britain again.

CHAPTER 5

There were about forty reporters, not counting television crews, in the Great Hall of Edinburgh Castle, awaiting the arrival of John Serjeant. It was only after we had arrived in the castle that we were told he would be addressing the Press Conference. No doubt his decision to visit Scotland was being kept secret for security reasons. The city had been occupied by the English troops the day before, the Scots having made no attempt to defend it, much to everyone's surprise. Daimyo tanks were still parked at street intersections, and Tartar armoured cars prowled around looking for signs of trouble, but so far not a shot had been fired. Those citizens that remained were prudently keeping indoors, but many of the buildings looked deserted. On our way to the castle we had seen a few people coming out of the temple of Saint Giles, but that had been the only sign of life.

I caught sight of the Affiliated Press man among the crowd and went to speak to him. He greeted me with surprise. "Hello! Where have you been? I thought I'd be seeing you in the Press convoy, but you weren't anywhere around."

"I managed to give the British liaison officer the slip", I replied, "and got myself hooked on to the Second Division - you know, the one that attacked through Gretna Green and Annandale."

"I thought that was top secret," said the AP man. "The Scots were certainly taken by surprise at Gretna. They expected the weight of the English thrust would be on the east coast. How did you find out about it, you cunning old bastard?"

"It was Bernie, my interpreter. He seems to have a way of persuading people to talk to him. While we're in here listening to a lot of eyewash he'll probably be finding out what's really going to happen next."

"I should think that's pretty obvious. Wouldn't you?" said the APman. "The Scots are bound to try and negotiate a settlement, now that they've been rolled back from all their defence lines. Whether or not Serjeant will listen to them is a different matter, though. Wouldn't you say so? It's been a pretty nasty five days and a hell of a lot of English soldiers won't be going home again."

"I suppose you're right", I replied, "But from what I've seen the Scottish army hasn't been destroyed yet. It was incredible, the way that Johnston pulled them out from between the English pincers at Musselburgh and Dalkeith. I heard that last night the First Division lost contact with their rearguard around Falkirk."

"The English are running short of fuel. That's the only reason they haven't pressed their pursuit," he said. "Once they've filled up their tanks again there'll be no holding them. The four Typhoons on their own should be enough to clinch it; and they've still got two helicopter gunships left."

"They're not very accurate, though, are they?" I commented. "I watched two of the Typhoons in action at Gretna. They blew most of the village to pieces; but when the English tanks finally pushed their way through and I followed them in, it didn't look as if a single foxhole or gun emplacement had been hit from the air. At best, I'd say, they helped by making the Scots keep their heads down. And the other four gunships didn't last long against the anti-aircraft missiles, did they?"

"So you think the Scots might still have a chance with some kind of counter-attack," said the AP man.

"I just wouldn't put it past Johnston to hold on for a bit longer if Serjeant doesn't offer them attractive terms," I said. "But I suppose a lot will depend on Knox's attitude, if he's still in control. I don't see him giving up easily."

"You've seen that character close-up, haven't you? What did you make of him?"

"I thought he was a bit cracked, in some way that I can't quite define. But he's as cunning as a cage of monkeys. And he seems to have the knack of making people believe in him."

Outside we heard the racket of a descending helicopter; and a couple of minutes later the double doors at the end of the hall were thrown open by two paratroopers armed with sub-machine-guns, who looked at us menacingly as the little entourage marched in with the great man in the centre.

Serjeant gave a short address in English to begin with, mainly for the benefit of his own radio people. The he read the rest of us a speech in Japanese. His pronunciation reminded me irresistibly of a slightly racist impression the old comedian, Kazuo Fukutake, used to do of an Antwerp University graduate newly arrived in Japan and anxious to impress with the extent of his Easternisation. It was an unfair comparison, but it kept coming into my mind as his white teeth flashed, although they seemed to be unco-ordinated with the expressionless blue eyes behind his large, round spectacles.

He had come, said Serjeant, to offer his personal congratulations to the armed forces on their magnificent achievement, and to see for himself the extent of the damage caused by the fighting. And he wanted also to reassure loyal Scots that they had nothing to fear. They would be given the full protection of the law, and every assistance they needed to get their province back to a state of normality.

"But," continued the Prime Minister, raising the index finger of his right hand and shaking it at the television cameras, "I must also take this opportunity to warn those who are persisting in their treason against the constitution of our great country that they must expect to encounter the full rigour of the law. The time is past when there can be talk of negotiations and arrangements. Too much blood has already been spilled to allow those who have inflicted these grievous wounds on the body of their own country to escape the consequences of their criminal recklessness."

At this the three senior officers standing behind Serjeant nodded their heads in vigorous agreement. He continued, "I would be failing in my duty to future generations if I were now, by acts of mistaken leniency, to encourage the belief that ambitious men can take up arms – and incite others to take up arms – against the unity of this nation, and then, when they fail in their object, be accepted back into society as if nothing had happened – indeed, as if they were deserving of some special consideration not accorded to lesser criminals. So long as I am head of this administration law will not talk with treason – except to pass sentence on it."

"He must be pretty confident that he's finally routed them," muttered the AP man.

Serjeant then said he would be happy to answer our questions. Immediately he was asked for his estimate of the military situation, and on this he deferred to the commanding officer, General Tettley, a stocky, wizened man, whose left arm had been put out of action fighting in the Japanese Army against the Turks at Gaza. He had reached the rank of major before Independence, and his final promotion had come when his predecessor was sacked after the Newcastle fiasco.

"Just a matter of mopping up," said Tettley. "The enemy has ceased to exist as an organized force. Of course, there may be a few pockets of resistance, especially if any of those Highland fellows get back to their native mountains. But we have what's needed to winkle them out, and we intend to show them we mean business."

I happened to glance in the direction of the door through which we had entered and caught a glimpse of Bernie talking to the sergeant on guard. Immediately I went over to them and the sergeant said, "This man has a message for a Mr. Hashimoto. Is that you?"

I assented, taking the folded piece of paper from his hand and opening it, I read, "Rioting in Caernarfon (Wales). Police station wrecked. Welsh independence gang. Bernie." I winked and nodded at Bernie over the sergeant's shoulder, and hurried back to the group.

Serjeant was telling them that the government planned to use the expected oil revenues for the good of the whole country, which would, of course, include Scotland. When he had finished speaking I asked, "Prime Minister, could we have your views on the rioting in Caernarfon (I hoped I had the pronunciation right) today? Do you see it as the beginning of a movement in Wales similar to what has been happening here in Scotland?"

His cold, blue eyes flickered with surprise and he glanced quickly at the group standing behind him. But then he seemed to recover his composure and said, "Ah... yes. Well, we've only just heard about this before coming here, and there really hasn't been time to obtain an assessment of the magnitude of the incident. However, I can say with confidence there is nothing happening in Wales which is in any way comparable with the deplorable events of the past six months. The Welsh Rifles played a magnificent part in the battles at Darlington and Musselburgh."

One of the officers whispered something in his ear. "I'm told that their Second Battalion is in the city today, and I'm sure that if any of you wanted to meet some of the officers and men that could be arranged. What has happened today is most likely a case of some hotheads exploiting a local grievance. But one thing you can be certain of – no one in Wales, looking at what is happening in Scotland, could possibly imagine that his own province – or he himself – could benefit from a repetition of these events."

There was a buzz of conversation among the journalists before the next question. The conference ended about ten minutes later, with Serjeant waving and smiling with all his teeth at the cameras, which he invited to accompany him on an inspection of the troops.

"I don't know about you," said the AP man as we walked to the door, "but I'm going to Wales. I smell a story. It was pretty sharp of your fellow to pick up that news so quickly."

"It wouldn't surprise me if he got it from Serjeant's radio operator," I said. "But I think I'll stay with the big story for a while longer. I didn't find Tettley very convincing."

"I find those convincing," said my companion, pointing to the sleek solidity of four Daimyo tanks parked below the castle wall.

Miranda rejoined me, camera in hand. "Did you get any good ones?" I asked her.

"He's not exactly photogenic," she replied. "A bit grey and uninteresting, and there's nothing I can do about that."

"I wonder if he would agree with what our famous revolutionary leader, Nobunaga, once said. He told a sycophantic painter, 'By leaving out my wrinkles you have robbed me of half my life.'" I put my hand on her waist and squeezed lightly, marvelling at its softness under my fingers. But I felt her shrink from my touch, just slightly, and saw her turn her face away to avoid my eyes.

We found Bernie and I congratulated him on the speed with which he had brought me the news. "Who told you about it?" I asked.

"The helicopter pilot," he replied. "I was telling him what a lovely landing he made. Does this mean we're going to be on the road to Wales?"

"No. I think we'll stay around here a bit longer – specially after that speech we've just heard. I can't see Knox and his boys just coming and turning themselves in. But do *you* think there's something big brewing up in Wales?"

Bernie shook his head. "I don't think so, captain. Those Welsh fellows are too poor to start a fight. From what I've heard they're living on top of each other in their valleys, with about enough good land to graze a goat for every family."

"A young fellow I travelled with on the plane, who reckoned he was an expert on the subject, wouldn't agree with you," I said. "He thought that those were just the kind of people who would start a revolution."

"Well, you can tell him from me that he's wrong," said Bernie. "If a fellow has never had time to think about anything except where his next meal is coming from he doesn't have time to start thinking about revolutions. It's the fellow who's got enough to be going on with that starts looking around at what some other fellow has and wondering how he can get his hands on a bit of it. And if he can see some private way of doing it, he'll give that a try – inside the law or outside it, according to what sort of fellow he is. But if all the private ways are blocked off then he might think of getting together with other fellows and having a revolution, to get them unblocked. See what I mean?"

"Yes," I said. "I wish you could have met this character on the plane. It would have been an interesting conversation to listen to."

Bernie had discovered that the Grand Central Railway Hotel, where he had hoped to lodge us, had been abandoned by its staff. Now, along with a dozen other journalists, and with the consent of the Army liaison officer, we moved in there to 'camp'. It was a vast, cavernous place, with marble tiled floors, dark panelling in the corridors and potted palms in unlikely corners – built a few years before the Transcontinental War, I would say. On the first floor we found quite a pleasant suite that was large enough to accommodate the three of us in a style to which we were totally unaccustomed.

While Miranda and I were getting unpacked and searching for candles in the room service pantry, Bernie went on an expedition to the kitchens. He returned laden like a packmule. "I reckon they'd been entertaining some of those Honanese oilmen," he said. "They've got in a better class of food than you'd normally expect to find in a place like this."

Of necessity, he had chosen a selection of cold dishes, but it was much the best meal we'd had in five days of living rough, and we ate hungrily. When we had finished Bernie stretched out on a pile of silk-covered cushions on the floor and fell asleep almost immediately.

Miranda looked at me across the debris-strewn table and smiled, and I thought I saw a flicker of that familiar glow in her eyes once again.

"Let's leave the washing-up," I said. She laughed, and I felt myself beginning to relax.

"What's the significance of the X?" I asked her, pointing to the elaborately carved fireplace, over the centre of which was a shield bearing the emblem I had seen on the Scottish flag. "Something to do with the national holy man, isn't it?"

"Yes," said Miranda, "It's the cross of Saint Andrew, the patron saint of Scotland."

"But why a cross?"

"I suppose it's because he was crucified on one," she said. "I don't really know the story."

"Oh, that kind of cross. Now I see. I knew about the Christian god being crucified, but I hadn't realised that there were others as well. It seems an odd kind of symbol – an instrument of torture."

"Yes, I've sometimes thought that," said Miranda. "My mother wasn't religious, but she sent me to a school that was run by nuns – because it was supposed to be good. They taught us a lot about religion, but I've forgotten most of it already. I wasn't very interested."

"Oddly enough, I *was* quite interested in it when I was at school," I said, "but unfortunately we were only taught about Buddhism. I wish now that I'd learnt a bit about Christianity and Islam and Hinduism as well. I've read a certain amount about them, of course, but not very much about Christianity, I'm afraid. Tell me, why does it claim to be monotheistic when it has three – or is it four – gods?"

Miranda shook her head. "We used to have lessons about that but I never really understood it. There was God the Father, who created everything, and God the Son – the one who was crucified - and the Holy Ghost, who was supposed to be all around us. But somehow they were all one person, and it was very wicked to believe anything else. People used to be killed for having other opinions about that.

"Down in Southern Europa, near where you've just been, some people called Albigensians used to have a different idea. They said that the Devil was nearly as powerful as God, and he was in control of the physical world, while God only ruled over what was spiritual. But the mainstream Christians massacred them in thousands and even burned them alive. That was before the Mongol Conquest. I learnt about it in a history lesson, not in religious instruction."

"What about the goddess – the one with the child, in all the pictures and statuettes?"

"You mean the Virgin Mary. She's not a goddess – although they do say prayers to her. She was the mother of Jesus – God the Son. She had him while she was still a virgin. The nicest of the Christian festivals is all about him being born, in a stable. It's called 'Christmas', and we have special food and give each other presents, and everybody tries to be kind and good-humoured for one day in the year."

"Yes, I think I've heard of that," I said. "The way that sex gets left out of the story interests me. Do you think it was because of this virgin birth idea that the Christian priests became so bothered about sex? Or were they bothered about it to begin with, and left it out because they wanted the story to back up their ideas?"

"I don't really know if there's a connection," Miranda replied. "But they do get very worked up about it… sex, I mean." She seemed to be forcing herself to say the word. "The nuns never actually said much about it – only hinted. But they managed to get across the idea that it was bad. There was a time, I remember, when I even thought it was wicked to look at my own body. When we got to be fourteen we had to wear long skirts, down to our ankles, and we were never allowed to show our bare arms."

"What an extraordinary idea!" I exclaimed. "You mean your body was something bad, that nobody should be allowed to look at?"

"That was the general idea. Don't religious people in Japan think like that?"

"No. As far as I know, they never have. We have public baths, for example, where men and women go in the water together."

Miranda's eyes were round with amazement. "The nuns weren't even very happy about private baths," she said. "I mean ones where you went in by yourself. I think that was how I got the idea that I shouldn't look at myself."

"I suppose the theory is that the sight of a naked body promotes desire, and desire is wicked," I said. "But it doesn't need much observation to see that that isn't true. Most people look a lot more desirable with a few clothes on." I was about to add, "With a body like yours, of course, it might be true," but I checked myself.

"But don't you think it becomes true if you start believing it? I mean, if everybody believed that bare hands were very naughty, and wore gloves all the time, then most people would get a thrill out of seeing somebody who wasn't wearing gloves. Don't you think so?"

"Yes, I think you're right. Maybe the more taboos we have the more exciting life becomes. But it gets more frustrating, too, I should think, and that can be dangerous."

Miranda nodded. "Even when I was at school I used to think they were getting things a bit out of proportion. I mean, old Knox is supposed to be a Christian, and however many people he kills the priests will still accept him, provided he makes his confessions. But if he was to divorce his wife – supposing he's married – and marry someone else they'd have nothing more to do with him. That doesn't make sense to me."

"Maybe it follows that if you start calling things that are good – like your own body – evil, after a while things that really are evil seem to matter less, or even begin to look good," I said. "I suppose the priests would have said it was good to kill all those people you were telling me about who didn't agree with their ideas on the nature of God."

"Oh, yes. They made it into a crusade. That meant the people who were doing the killing would go straight to heaven if they happened to get killed themselves." Looking down at the carpet to avoid my eyes, she went on, "It's easy to talk rationally about good and evil, like we're doing now, when nothing's actually happening – when you're not under pressure, I mean. Then you can think clearly and make up your mind for yourself. But when something goes wrong, or you're all on your own – in the middle of the night, maybe – the old ideas they pumped into you when you were a child seem to take over. It's not easy to get away from feelings that are deep down inside you."

I was sure that she was trying to tell me something about the reason for her change of attitude after the rape attempt, but equally certain that she didn't want to talk about it openly. Maybe, incredible though it seemed to me, the episode had uncovered beneath her Easternized sophistication a deep-rooted belief that sexual desire was evil and nasty, and a sin against the Christian god. Whatever the source of the trouble might be, I knew I would have to tread lightly if I wasn't to frighten her back behind the wall of silence. If I could keep the conversation on sex, but not in a way that would make her feel threatened, she might eventually, I hoped, relax enough to confide in me.

"I'm sure it isn't," I said. "It must be very difficult for young people here who have Eastern ideas about marriage not to feel guilty if they choose their own husbands or wives, and don't let their parents make the choice for them."

"You don't have arranged marriages in Japan, do you?" she asked.

"No, not nowadays. But it was once the rule for most people. I suppose things started changing when industrialization broke up the old family system. But I don't think there's any evidence to show that marriages are happier now than they were then just because of that particular change. It's the change in the status of women that has made the biggest difference. In the old days I don't think anyone would even have asked whether a woman was happy in her marriage. It was her job to make her husband happy, and at best he was expected to treat her kindly."

"That's how it still is here, for most people," said Miranda. "In theory we have equality for women, but that's an Eastern idea and the men don't really believe in it."

"What about the women?" I asked.

"Oh, I know a lot of people say that the women are even more against equality than the men, but I don't believe that it's true. It's just that most of them have never even heard of the idea. You know, more than half of them can't read. I don't mean that they're all unhappy, or that some of them don't manage to rule the roost at home. And it's a bit better in the towns now, where a lot of the girls go out to work if they can get a job – though it can't be much fun working ten hours a day in one of those big factories. But at least they've got some independence.

"It's the girls in the country I really feel sorry for. They work in the house and in the fields when they're not at school – if they ever get the chance to go to school – and they're not allowed to be seen around with boys. And then, sometimes when they're only sixteen, their parents get rid of them to some man, with a couple of pigs or a cow thrown in to make him think he's getting a bargain. And after that they belong to him. They depend on him completely for everything they want. And every year almost, unless they're lucky, there's another baby, so that they're old and worn out by the time they're thirty.

"If the husband's a good man I suppose there can be love, and that makes it bearable. I'll say this for the priests – they do at least preach that the husbands ought to treat their wives kindly. But if the husband isn't good he can beat and abuse the poor woman and there's nothing she can do about it. And the chances are she'll watch two or three of her children die, because if they catch anything there won't be a doctor out in the country. Who wouldn't want to change that kind of existence, if they knew there was any alternative?"

"Who wouldn't?" I agreed. "But I'm afraid that's not what women in Japan think about when they talk of women's rights."

"Well, I suppose they have their own problems," said Miranda. "But I'm one of the very few lucky ones here. My mother had enough money to give me an education. She didn't have old-fashioned ideas. And then – I still don't know how it happened – I got a job that I really wanted to do. When I see other women – like the two we saw yesterday carrying their children back into that burnt out village – it makes me feel guilty. It really does." There was a seriousness in her eyes that I had never seen there before.

"Why feel guilty?" I said. "I expect that's something else you learnt from the nuns. But it wasn't you that made those women miserable, and you don't want to keep them that way. And you haven't been indifferent to them either. Feel compassion. Feel anger. But don' t waste your time on guilt. It's a dreary, negative emotion - a kind of spiritual self-indulgence. I can understand it being popular with people who spend their time praying to an instrument of torture."

"But don't you ever feel ashamed of things you've done?" she asked.

"Shame? That's a different matter," I replied. "Of course I feel ashamed when I realize I've done something wrong, something I oughtn't to have done. And then - I hope - I try to put it right, or if I can't, I try to remember not to do it again. But I don't let shame grow into guilt. Guilt is a bad motive to rely on.

“Give your guilt to the nuns and let them pray about it. You go on taking good pictures, to show that you've deserved your luck. And if there's something more you ought to be doing to help those other women, do it.”

"That's the trouble," she said. "I'm sure there are other things I ought to be doing but I don't know what they are. And sometimes I don't think I'm the person to do them, anyway. There have been times when I wanted to be a nun - only I couldn't believe all the religious stuff. It's guilt that keeps getting in the way. One part of me wants to do things that another part thinks are wrong and disgusting. And you can't really help other people if you don't know what's right and what's wrong yourself.”

"Is that really what's bothering you, or might it be that you're able to feel for yourself what's right but other people have told you, very persuasively, that it's wrong.”

She looked at me with wide, troubled eyes. "All our ideas about right and wrong come to us from other people," she said. "What we have to do is to choose between them. But it's harder to think clearly about ideas you were given when you were very young, especially if they've got tied up with your feelings as well. I don' t suppose you can understand what I 'm talking about - you never seem to let your feelings interfere with what you're doing."

"If you knew how often they do interfere you'd be surprised. I think I can understand."

"We were taught that sex was for having babies, and nothing else," she said, suddenly determined, it seemed, to speak what was in her thoughts. "Of course, I didn't believe that when I got to be a bit older, and read a few Eastern books. But my mother never talked about it. And then I couldn't help noticing all the trouble it causes. Maybe the trouble comes because, like you said, if people make lots of rules they want to break them; and I suppose it's breaking the rules that really causes most of the trouble. But then when it happens… when you see for yourself... What do *you* think sex is for?"

"I think it's for having babies, and for fun – which was the bait that nature put on the hook to ensure that people would go to all the trouble of having babies - and for getting closer to somebody you love. And the last of those, I'd guess, came after we'd developed language. I don't think it's instinctive. It's probably one of the foundations we built our civilizations on."

"But do you think it's right to have it for one reason, without the others as well?" she said.

"Only a Westerner would ask a question like that," I replied, with a smile. "No, I suppose that's not quite true. There must be other parts of the world where they worry about that kind of thing, too. Yes, I do think it's right. And whether it's right or not, I suspect that's what happens most of the time. More important - it's *possible* nowadays, since we've got the birth tablets, and all the other kinds of contraceptives."

"I wasn't thinking so much about the having babies part of it," said Miranda, "though I know that's the most important part, really. But you said about getting close to somebody you love. Could you do it for that with somebody, and just for fun with somebody else?"

"Why not?" I said. "After all, what are we talking about? - a series of physical sensations, shared by two people. Provided they've made sure that there's no baby as a result, what difference does it make to anyone? A conversation like we're having now could have more life-changing consequences than sharing an erotic experience for a few minutes. Of course, if they want some kind of long-term relationship the sex act starts to take on whatever meaning they choose to give it.

"But that's very different from the old idea that you still find traces of, even in Japan, that the woman is the man's property, and if anyone else copulates with her he's stealing. And in that situation duty is supposed to demand that she doesn't allow herself to be 'stolen' - and so you get the basis for all those novels and plays that modern audiences can't identify with any longer. Nowadays we just can't share the feelings of the people they were written for."

"But don't you think there's any right or wrong in it?" she asked.

"Oh, yes. I do. I think it's wrong to have sex if both people aren't getting something out of it." I was going to add, "It's a kind of rape," but again I checked myself.

"They might not both be getting the same thing, but it'll

probably be better if they are. I don't think I could get much fun out of it if the other person wasn't doing it for fun as well - but then I don't suppose everybody's like that. But if the other person doesn't really want to do it - if you've bribed, or bullied or deceived her into it, then you're only using her and - though I know we do it all the time - I think using people is wrong. Does that make sense to you?"

She nodded. "Yes, it does. With my head I think you're right, but there's a lot of difference between the theory and what you feel deep down. I don't know how you can change your feelings."

"It's not easy," I agreed. "Maybe one day people won't be forced to waste so much time worrying about sex, and will just get on with enjoying it. I sometimes think that sex for fun is the kind that causes least trouble, even if it is more exciting when you're doing it for love. Love can so quickly become possessive.

"I suppose that's where those deep-rooted feelings about sex come in again through the back door, when we think we've thrown them out of the window. If people could only stop getting worked up about the rights and wrongs of sex they might have more feelings to spare for things like love and beauty, and pain and poverty - things that really matter."

"Do you think that will ever happen?" asked Miranda.

"I think it's already begun - certainly in my country," I said, "And now that people don't need to worry about having babies if they don't want them, the whole thing may start falling into perspective - just like those problems that looked so big when we were children, and somehow seemed to shrink when we got a bit older."

"People in this country still have to worry. We made birth control illegal last year. It's even against the law to talk about it."

"Yes. I'd forgotten," I said. "The priests have been doing a bit of counter-attacking with the help of their friends in politics. And from their own point of view they're quite right. Anything that reduces fear – and that means reducing guilt - has got to be a threat to religion."

"That's the difference between this country and yours," said Miranda. "Here most people believe that the past is more important than the future, even though they pretend they're trying to get away from the past. But in reality they're trying to get back into it. That's why I don't think you can really understand what it's like to have feelings that were planted deep down inside you long before you knew that you didn't want them."

Her brown eyes were dull and despondent. I got up and stood behind her. "I don't think we're all that different," I said, putting my hands on her shoulders, and pressing the firm flesh gently beneath my fingers. "Even if I can't understand, I can feel the pain that it gives you. But I'm sure the pain will pass, because you're not a life-hater."

"How do you mean?" she asked, and I felt her shoulders relax a little. Moving the tips of my fingers lightly towards her neck, I began slowly to massage her. "It's a theory I have - totally unscientific and based purely on personal observation. I think people come in two varieties. There are those who are never happy unless they're being negative - opposing, complaining about something, putting somebody down. They're the kind that guilt can really get hold of, but they're probably better at coping with disappointment. I call them the life-haters.

“The life-lovers are happier building things up than pulling them down, and they'd sooner sit in the sun than go looking for trouble. And when trouble comes they don't moan about it: they try to get rid of it. But they're sometimes a bit slow at noticing when things start going wrong.

“I expect it takes both kinds to keep the world moving, but I'd rather be a life-lover. And I'm pretty certain that you're one. That's why I believe those old guilt feelings haven't got such strong roots as you think they have. A bit of sunshine will wither them up."

She bent her head back and looked up into my face. "I hope you're right. It helps to talk about things."

I bent towards her, intending to kiss her lightly on the forehead, but she jerked her head to avoid my lips and stood up.

"I must go to bed now," she said. "It's been such a long day. If I'm not up by seven, wake me with sweet music."

She walked across the wide room with that graceful movement of her hips that I used to dream about in Provence, and for once I was glad that she couldn't know the fierce longing that was welling up inside me as I watched her go.

CHAPTER 6

The grey rooftops of the town of Perth, rising above the river mist, were a welcome sight on the chill autumn morning. We had had an uneasy passage through the night on our voyage from Musselburgh. Both Bernie and Miranda had been seasick, and I had felt queasy more than once myself. The skipper of the little fishing vessel – the only one I could find that boasted an engine – had been jumpy all the way, fearing that we might be sighted by a government patrol boat and fired on as a blockade runner (which, in a sense, we were). So it was a relief to be in the calmer waters of the Tay and chugging steadily through the mist with our destination coming into view.

Now that it was nearly over, the boat trip seemed an absurdly simple way of getting around the embattled zone that divided Scotland along the Carse of Forth. It felt like a very long time since that optimistic press conference in Edinburgh Castle, although it was, in fact, only five weeks. But the mopping-up operation predicted by Tettley had never taken place. In two days, while the government forces were recovering their wind and bringing up supplies of fuel and ammunition, Johnston had regrouped his battered army. Then he had counter-attacked fiercely at Stenhousemuir, while a raiding party was working its way round Tettley's left flank. The raiders had struck near Linlithgow, causing chaos by destroying a supply convoy, and had then disappeared into the Pentland Hills.

The setback to the Army's advance had been only temporary, but it had undermined confidence, and from that time onward Tettley moved much more cautiously. A week later he was ready to recover the lost ground, but two more raids on his communications, at Moffat and just outside Berwick on Tweed, diverted several battalions to the rear. When he finally moved against Stirling the Scots were firmly dug in, and the wire-guided anti-tank missiles that had just been added to their armoury proved highly effective against the Daiymos. Three days of hard slogging, which we watched from near Tettley's headquarters in the village of Bannockburn, showed that the Scots were very far from being defeated. Without armour, aircraft or heavy artillery, however, they were unable to exploit any temporary advantage that they gained.

After a week's lull in the fighting the government forces tried an out-flanking movement, crossing the Forth about ten miles higher up. But Johnston had anticipated them, and they ran into a costly ambush. Another lull was followed by another expensive frontal attack, when the southerners finally battered their way into the smouldering ruins of Stirling, losing half their remaining armour in the process. But the victory was a hollow one, for they failed to establish a bridgehead across the river, whence the Scots had withdrawn to carefully prepared positions.

It was this situation of stalemate that had led me to think once again of crossing the lines and finding out what was going on in the rebel camp. Knox had made Perth his seat of government, and so it was to Perth that I finally decided to go.

There were few people around when we berthed alongside a wooden landing-stage, and our arrival seemed to cause little curiosity. When we had just finished paying the skipper his second instalment and collecting our luggage a young corporal, carrying a rifle, came running along the landing stage towards us. Bernie told him who we were, and that we wanted to see Major Mackie, whom he described as an old friend of ours. At first the man seemed puzzled, but then he exclaimed, "*Colonel* Mackie," and immediately directed Bernie to where the Colonel could be found. Knox's entourage had taken over a venerable inn called 'The Salutation', and there we found Mackie in a small room on the first floor, sitting on his bed and pulling on his boots. He seemed genuinely pleased to see us, and sprang up to greet us with an effusive mixture of Eastern bows and Western handshakes. Once again, I discovered, I was the only reporter on the Scottish side of the lines, apart from a Honanese television crew.

An interview with Knox was arranged for the afternoon, and we spent the rest of the morning looking around the town. It was a pleasant place, with the broad river flowing through, and looked cleaner than many of the towns I had seen farther south, even if there were fewer signs of modernization. Perhaps it lacked the attractions that drew in the squatters to other places in such great numbers.

Recent arrivals of a different kind were much in evidence, however. As well as the people around the administration, whose vehicles were continually throwing the narrow streets of the town centre into confusion, we found a tented camp for refugees near the riverside. Miranda took some interesting photographs, especially of the children, whose favourite game was 'English and Scots'. The inmates were nearly all women and children, with a few old men, and they seemed in reasonably good physical shape, although the adults had an air of restless anxiety about them. The male refugees, Mackie later informed us, had all been recruited for military duties of one kind or another.

When we were leaving the refugee camp I caught sight of an Eastern face in one of the tents and went to investigate. It belonged to a monk from Kyushu, who introduced himself as Osamu Okamoto and walked with us back to the town centre. He had been the headmaster of a mission school in Falkirk, and when the townspeople, most of whom were Buddhists, had decided to flee to the north before the advancing English, he had come with them.

"It was a long march," said Osamu, "but we didn't lose a single one of them on the way." I sensed from the note of pride in his voice that he had played a part in the organization. Some of the refugees, he told us, had gone to a large camp in Dunfermline, but he had chosen to accompany this group to Perth.

"They're simple souls," he said, "and frightened to be so far from their homes. For them coming up here is almost like moving to another country. It's so close to the Highlands, and they're almost as afraid of the Highlanders as they are of the English. But if this war has a successful outcome it may finally get rid of all the old divisions. It could be the making of Scotland in more ways than one."

Astonished by his enthusiasm, I asked, "Do you really think the Scots have a chance of winning the war, and keeping their independence?"

"Certainly they have," he replied, "if only the Japanese government would keep out of it and stop pumping arms into London. But maybe the weight of world public opinion will do something about that. You see, these Scots are a people who take kindly to discipline. It's a hard country they have, not unlike Kyushu in places – but colder, of course – and it makes them realistic. The bright boys in my school want to be engineers or doctors. You take a similar bunch of lads in a school down south and you'll find that half of them want to be lawyers. The southerners think that being educated means not getting your hands dirty."

"But if the Scots are so able why didn't they do well for

themselves in the united republic?" I asked.

"Oh, many of them did indeed – as individuals – especially under Japanese rule. But after Independence I think racial jealousy was beginning to play a part, and the best man didn't always get the job. What the Scots lacked most, however, was capital to develop their own province – their own country; and that's what the oil can give them. They don't need the union any more, even though it may be the worse without them."

"What do you think of Knox?" I asked.

"I've only seen him once," said Osamu, "when he visited the camp last week. I suppose he's a bit of a fire-eater, but he didn't strike me that way. More of an idealist, I'd say – a man of vision. You know, even in the midst of all the fighting he has taken time to concern himself with questions like the revival of national culture and moral reform. Like all these Christians, he's perhaps a little preoccupied with sexual morality at the expense of more important matters; but it's all part of a great tradition of restraint and respect for authority. I feel there is a great deal that the West can teach us, if we study its ways with an open mind."

"What about the supply situation?" I enquired. "Is there going to be enough food – in your own camp for instance?"

He nodded his dark, round head seriously. "It's a worrying problem," he said. "We have pretty strict rationing now, and so far supplies are holding out well. Most people are used to a pretty simple diet – oatmeal porridge, a few vegetables, milk, cheese, fish and a piece of meat now and again. They can get by on that. But the province always has to import food, especially since the population began increasing so rapidly; and all these people in the towns can't grow their own food. I hear that some supplies have been coming in from Scandinavia, but the Navy turned back a ship bound for Aberdeen last week. And some oats have been getting to the west coast from Ireland, but the harvest hasn't been good there this year. Of course it hasn't been at all good in Scotland – what with the rain, and men away at the war, and now the lowland crop falling into the hands of the southerners. If the war continues into the winter we're going to need help."

We parted from Osamu at the town hall, where the Scottish government had found a temporary home. Mackie was waiting to take

Miranda and me into the office of the Chancellor, as Knox was now calling himself. As before, the great man was wearing a kilt, but this time his jacket was of black velvet, and pinned on the left breast he had an elaborate brooch which I took to be some kind of order or decoration. On the wall behind his chair hung a yellow banner depicting a red lion standing on its hind legs.

"Aha! My young friends from the *Nagoya Guardian*!" he exclaimed as we entered, and waved a podgy hand for us to be seated. "You have come because you know where the news is to be found. Let me tell you something. My father was only a humble laird, but he was a very astute man, and people used to say of him, 'You never see Tom Knox at a hole if there isn't a rat in it.' You have something of that quality, I think, young man." He beamed at me.

"Thank you – Chancellor," I said. "May I ask why this new title has been chosen for your office?"

He seemed pleased to have been asked. "A very intelligent question. It has been chosen to revive what was once the highest office of the ancient Kingdom of Scotland. You will know from your history, I am sure, that Scotland once held a proud place among the nations of the West and never yielded to any – until your own valiant people, with their superior weaponry, incorporated her into the Empire. But even they saw fit not to tamper with many of the ancient ways. Those splendid Highlanders you have seen in our battle line have ordered their own affairs with little interference since the time of the old kings. We have a deep respect in Scotland for our old traditions. You know, my own father was descended on his mother's side from the great House of Canmore, that once provided this country with its kings."

"How very interesting," I said. "It's remarkable that, with all the problems you have confronting you, you still find time to think of these matters of tradition."

"You are very observant, young man." He leaned forward confidentially. "What you may not realize is that these matters have an important bearing on the problems we are facing. Tradition is our secret weapon. It gives us the will to resist and the will to conquer; and for that reason we have to preserve and strengthen it."

"Would you say that morale is high among your people?" I asked.

"It couldn't be higher. We have given the English a bloody nose; and before very long, when our strength has been built up, we will sweep them from the sacred soil of Scotland, never to return."

"Are you expecting, then, to receive supplies of arms from outside sources?"

He laid a fat forefinger along the side of his large nose and winked at me conspiratorially. "We both know that that's not a question I can answer," he said, "but you're a sharp lad and you can draw your own conclusions."

I smiled and nodded. "What about food supplies, Chancellor?" I asked. "I understand that you have introduced a system of rationing."

"It is a precaution which we have felt to be in the interests of the poorer classes," he replied. "At such a time of uncertainty it is to be expected that prices might rise and those without money would go short. And, of course, the presence of a large number of refugees from the temporarily occupied territory has created a certain pressure on supplies."

"But you don't anticipate any shortage this winter?"

He pursed his lips and looked serious. "A great deal could happen before the winter. But let me say just this – if the English think they can use the weapon of starvation against our people they are greatly mistaken. We have resources upon which to draw that they know nothing of. Write what I have told you," he added, wagging his finger at me, "so that they may be under no misapprehension."

"So you won't be making any appeal to overseas countries for food?" I asked.

"Young man," he said, again assuming his confidential manner, "it has always been a rule of my life to say only what I believe to be true. I could not now say to our many friends in other countries that we need food, knowing that our supplies are adequate. Of course, if gifts of food are sent we shall accept them gratefully, and employ them to ease the lot of the refugees. But what we need from our friends is the sinews of war. Once her enemies have been expelled Scotland will need no help from anyone. And when that time comes she will not forget those who have helped her in her hour of need."

He was clearly not going to be drawn on the military situation, except to reiterate his confidence, and to say that recruits had been flocking to the army from the Highlands. But when I mentioned the admiration that Johnston's generalship had won I saw what I thought to be a flicker of annoyance cross his face. Then he drew back his lips in a smile and said, "Scotland has been fortunate in her warrior sons, and not least in General Johnston. He has played a notable part in our victories and we honour him – as we honour our other brave sons. Colonel Mackie, Brigadier Cameron, the Earl of Mar and the Lord of the Isles have all played their parts nobly. The army will never want for fine leaders."

He stood up and, seeing Miranda begin to prepare her camera, smiled benevolently at her, nodding his head. "You know," he said, as he posed for the first photograph, "I'm an old military man myself, and I've always thought that a country which takes for its foundations the military virtues can surmount any obstacle. It is for that reason I welcome this time of testing, in which every man and woman – yes, and even the children – will have to stand firm in the ranks as warriors in the fight for freedom."

Turning to present his porcine profile to the lens, he continued, "The habits of discipline and steadfastness that they will learn will stand the nation in good stead when happier times return. My own character, as you know, has been moulded in the fires of conflict. It makes me very humble to think how much of those great qualities of leadership and decision-making I owe to the men who trained me in the old Imperial Army. You know, young man, the attributes of greatness may be born in us, but we need the help of other people to discover them and draw them out. That thought keeps me humble when men try to flatter me."

There was a knock on the door and Colonel Mackie entered. He went up to Knox and whispered to him. Knox's eyes gleamed with delight behind his spectacles, and he turned to me, saying, "Our young friend will be interested to hear this piece of news. Another success for our brave fighting men. We have just heard that the Long Range Striking Force has captured the town of East Linton and blown up the railway bridge – a catastrophic blow to the English communications. And so much, you will observe, for their claim to hold the half of Scotland. They don't even hold the railway."

"May I ask who commands the Striking Force?" I said.

Mackie replied, "Major Elliot, a man who was born and bred in the Borders."

"Aha!" said Knox, raising a podgy hand, "you're wrong, you know. I see Colonel Mackie's surprised that I say he's wrong. He doesn't often make mistakes."

"I'm sorry," said Mackie, looking bewildered. "I thought Elliot was in command."

"Ah, yes," said Knox, rubbing his hands in delight, "but you said *Major* Elliot. He's Colonel Elliot – I've promoted him."

"Oh. I didn't know that," said Mackie.

"You couldn't have known. I've just done it this very moment." Knox chuckled with glee, and Mackie laughed – a hearty, sycophantic laugh.

"We must send him his new insignia," said Knox. "Get a volunteer to take it through the lines to him. And we'll send a pennon to the Striking Force as well." He turned to me. "The fire in men's bellies is kindled by little sparks like that, young man."

We left the two of them in great good humour, having been promised a visit to the front line the following day. Outside Bernie rejoined us, and I said, "We'll go to the front tomorrow, but I doubt if there'll be much happening there. Afterwards I'd like to slip down to the south again and see if we can find this man Elliot and his bold Borderers."

"Not in that boat?" asked Bernie.

I laughed. "No. I think we might see if somebody can show us a way across the Forth, higher up, so that we can go around the flanks. I'm not sure what we could use for transport, but I expect you'll find something."

So it came about that, after we had visited the Scottish army's positions, with Colonel Mackie acting as our guide, and had admired the skill with which Johnston had prepared his defences, I made some enquiries about the Long Range Striking Force. At first Mackie was reluctant to give me any precise information, but eventually I persuaded him that I could be trusted not to talk to the English. Then he told me that if I went to the town of Selkirk I might find somebody who could arrange a meeting with Elliot – but there was no certainty that I would ever catch up with him, because he was constantly moving around.

In the little town of Dunblane, some way behind the lines, Bernie discovered that the blacksmith owned several donkeys and was prepared to hire them. After long negotiations the man was persuaded not only to let us ride three of his donkeys, but also to come with us and show where to cross the river. It was partly the size of the fee – modest in comparison with the price of an air line ticket, but the equivalent of a month's earnings to him – that decided him, but also a desire to make sure that his donkeys returned safely.

In the late evening we began the journey on our long-eared mounts. Miranda looked more comfortable riding side-saddle than I felt, dangling my legs without stirrups, only a thin blanket between me and the donkey's bony back. Some four hours later we arrived, stiff and bruised, at a tiny hamlet near the foot of the Lennox Hills, where the blacksmith's cousin lived.

At first sight of us the cousin and his wife were a little alarmed, but when they heard who we were their hospitality was warm and kindly. They fed us on porridge and made up a bed for Bernie and me on straw in the outhouse, while Miranda was given somebody's bed in the house. In the morning they seemed almost reluctant to take our money when we left them and set out on foot for the government forces' headquarters in Bannockburn, where we had left the Rough Rider.

CHAPTER 7

The last stretch of the road from Galashiels to Selkirk wound steeply upward, and the Rough Rider was as good as its name, bouncing over the uneven surface without breaking our bones, or its own back axle. But we were still a little tender from the donkey-ride of two days before, and I saw Miranda wince as she came down after a teeth-rattling toss.

"Is your bottom still sore?" I asked.

"I'll say it is," she replied. "They won't get me into the cavalry." And the merriment in her eyes was so unfeigned and carefree I began to hope that she was free again from the dark memories that had been clouding them. I returned her smile and shifted very slightly in my seat, so that my arm brushed against hers. Her body felt relaxed. Immediately my mind began to turn over plans that had lain disused and almost forgotten since the disaster at York. How could I begin to express the physical tenderness I felt for her without once again frightening her back behind her defences?

My pleasurable plotting was short-lived. Even before I saw what was in front I felt Miranda stiffen and shudder. Across the road ahead was a primitive barrier of logs and behind it stood four men, dressed in working clothes but wearing blue and white brassards on their left arms. One held a rifle, another had a large axe over his shoulder, and two were armed with bows and arrows.

"Don't worry," I said. "It's just an outpost. They'll have some discipline." I sounded confident, but now that we were back in this too-familiar situation I was far from certain that I had been sensible in bringing Miranda with us.

Bernie spoke to the sentries and clearly had some difficulty in understanding their reply. Then he produced a letter of introduction that Colonel Mackie had given us and held it out to them. The man with the rifle came round the barricade and took it from him, scrutinizing it at arm's length while Bernie went on talking. I guessed that the man couldn't read, but he may have been impressed by the symbol of the white cross on a blue shield, for he handed back the letter and spoke to his companions, who began to relax again. The man with the rifle even gave us a clumsy salute as we drove away.

"He says we should go to the courthouse in the middle of the town and ask for Willie Armstrong," said Bernie.

We passed an ancient watchtower (or such I presumed it to be) as we entered the town, and then came out into a wide market square. "That'll be the courthouse, I suppose," said Bernie, nodding his head towards a square, stone building which still had a chrysanthemum emblem in low relief over its doorway.

"They don't seem to have got far with de-colononization here," I remarked.

"Probably never got far with colonization, either," said Bernie.

There was a sentry at the door, armed with a long spear, and after producing the letter again we were taken inside to see Armstrong. He was a tall, scraggy, black-haired man with a long face and piercing blue eyes, who wore a green army tunic with grey woollen trousers and long boots that came above his knees. His Japanese was minimal and so Bernie conducted the interview.

Armstrong described himself as 'Cornet of the Selkirk Muster' and acknowledged that Elliot was his commander-in-chief. The Striking Force was in Ettrick Forest, he said, lying low after the raid on East Linton. Government planes and helicopters had been over several times the previous day, searching for the raiders. If we were prepared to wait around for a day, or maybe two days, it might be possible to arrange something. We could stay at an inn called 'The Fleece' just across the square. And in the meantime, he asked us to put our car under cover, because it might attract attention from the air.

Through Bernie I asked him if there had been any English soldiers in the neighbourhood. He laughed, harshly, and said that no English soldier would dare to come into those hills. When I enquired how many men he had under his command he replied that there were two hundred and twenty. Fifty of them had firearms. (His own Japanese Service revolver lay on the table in front of him.) One of the main duties of his Muster, I learned, was to help keep the Striking Force supplied with food – for the men and for the horses.

Armstrong accompanied us to the door of the courthouse, and when he saw the Rough Rider he wanted to examine it more closely. He had once driven a car, he said. So Bernie explained the controls to him and allowed him to drive us slowly to a stable yard, where the vehicle was parked in a hayshed. Then we returned to the inn, and had a meal of wheaten bread, cheese, milk and apples. Food was scarce, we were told, and nothing had come into the town for several weeks. However, we ate enough to fill us, and it was wholesome.

Bernie wanted to check over the car before it got dark. Since our mishap on the journey to York he had been almost obsessively careful, testing and re-testing everything at the beginning and end of each journey. We went with him to the stable yard, and then Miranda and I walked on to the edge of the town, because it was such a beautiful evening. The sky was clear and deep blue in the sinking sun, with just a few white clouds drifting lazily overhead. We stopped and leaned on a dry stone wall, looking downhill across a wide field that had been harvested and now lay empty, its surface warmly patterned in brown and yellow. In a tree not far away a bird was singing – a pure, melodious whistling. Miranda said it was a blackbird.

I put my arm around her shoulders and said, "Do you know, I think this is the first moment I've had to admire your country since I came here? With beautiful scenery like this it's a pity the sun doesn't shine more often."

"I think you've been a bit unlucky this year," Miranda replied. "We do sometimes have long, hot summers, and even in the winter it can be bright and crisp. I wish I'd travelled more, so that I knew how Britain compares with other places."

"For quiet, gentle beauty, with just a hint of wildness over the next hill I haven't seen anything better than this," I said. Then I turned from looking across the hilly landscape and fixed my eyes on the gentle curve of her cheek, the soft fullness of her lips and the graceful sweep of her long eyelashes. "Come to think of it, I could use exactly the same words to describe you."

She was silent for a moment and then, without turning her head, she asked, "Even the bit about wildness?"

All the cautious plans I had been making were blotted out of my mind. I couldn't wait a moment longer to put my hopes to the test. Slowly I drew my hand down her back until it came to rest on the softness of her hip. "If I was allowed to explore those hills I think I'd find out where the wildness is. I know it's there – and I think it's likely to be that much fiercer and more splendid because the surface is so calm and gentle."

"Do you really think so?" Her brown eyes were only

centimetres away from mine and they looked at me with an expression I hadn't seen in them before. "I've been thinking a lot about myself since we had that talk in Edinburgh." She paused, and I felt my stomach muscles tighten as I waited for the clue that would tell me whether or not I was going to succeed.

"You may be right about the wildness," she went on, "though I don't suppose it's the word I'd have used myself. But I think I *am* one of your 'life-lovers' – I know I want to be. And I've been thinking something else, too. When you went away to Provence I pretended to myself that I didn't care, but really I did. Now I've been thinking how lucky I am that you've come back, because you've helped me to find out about myself."

"Would you like to find out about the wildness, too?" I asked, my heart beginning to beat faster.

Her face was radiant with the vitality that had fascinated me the first time I saw her. "Yes, I think I would," she said softly.

I put my hand behind her slender neck and gently drew her face towards mine until our lips met. Her mouth was as soft and warm as I had expected it to be, and much more eager. After a moment of delight I drew back to look in her eyes again. They were shining with an unfeigned pleasure, and I needed no further reassurance.

Miranda was no stranger to kissing, at least, and she had a cunning tongue to reinforce the sensuous subtlety of her lips. After minutes of timeless enjoyment I reluctantly released her mouth and said, "My love, this is a beautiful place to be, but there are things I want to do that would outrage the natives. Will you come back with me to the inn?"

"Oh, yes," she said, shyly. And then, as we turned to go, she laughed and exclaimed, "I'm not going to pretend anymore – not even to myself. Let's walk quickly. I've been waiting so long, and now I don't want to wait any more."

I took her hand, slender and cool, as we walked, but she said, "I don't think the natives would like even that," and so I let it go again. There were only two old men in the main street when we turned into it, but I was conscious of other eyes that I couldn't see.

No one was around when we entered 'The Fleece', and as we climbed the creaking wooden stairway I asked, "Will you come to my room?" To have gone to hers would have been a surer way of avoiding any change of mind, but even now, with my body on fire for her, I wanted her to be certain of what she was doing.

"Yes, please," she answered, without hesitation, and her face was radiant. "I won't be long," she whispered, pushing on the heavy oak door to her own room, which was just across the landing from mine.

Rapidly I wrote a note and put it in Bernie's room, sticking it in the frame of the cracked mirror that hung on the wall. It said simply, "Gone to bed. See you in the morning." Then I hurried back to my own room and searched my wallet for a little packet of condoms that had travelled with me on all my journeys. I had carried them more as a talisman against despair than in any real expectation of using them. Indeed, I had never used one before, for both my late wife and the only other girl with whom I had ever made love had – like most other Japanese girls – been taking the birth tablet. Now I was anxious lest my inexperience with the condom might make me less able to deal gently with Miranda's virginity, but I couldn't take chances with her.

Hurriedly, and with a little fumbling, I stripped off my clothes and pulled on the ultra-lightweight dressing gown – black with red dragons leaping around on it – that was one of the few unnecessary items in my luggage. I was tying the sash when there was a light tap on the door and it groaned on its ancient hinges. Miranda entered, wearing her white, belted raincoat.

"I didn't bring a dressing gown," she said, smiling shyly. Her eyes were still shining. She had pulled the belt tight, emphasising the slenderness of her waist. I slipped my left arm around her and with my right hand pushed the heavy iron bolt on the door.

"We're not at home to visitors this evening," I said. Our two heads moved at the same instant, so that our lips met almost violently. This time her mouth felt familiar. Her arms were around me and I felt her fingers caressing my shoulders and stroking my spine. For a moment I withdrew my lips from hers and gently kissed the tip of her nose.

"I wnat to see all the beauty I've been so close to for so long," I whispered. "It's been like waiting for the clouds to lift from Mount Fuji." Then I kissed her again on her eyes and cheeks while my fingers found the buckle of her belt and undid it. Quickly I unbuttoned the raincoat and slipped both my hands inside to find the soft hemispheres of her breasts. She gave a little gasp as my fingers touched them, and I looked intently at her face. Her eyes were closed, but her lips were parted in a curve of contentment.

I bent my head and lightly kissed both nipples. She gasped again at each kiss. Then I covered her mouth once more with mine, and felt the tip of her tongue come thrusting between my teeth. Gently I slid my hands over the smooth skin of her shoulders and pushed the raincoat downward, easing it over her arms until it dropped to the floor. I stepped backward and looked at the loveliness revealed.

"You're making me shy," she said, lowering her eyelashes demurely and folding her hands in front of the dark triangle of black, curly hair. I laughed and drew her close to me, pressing my cheek against hers.

"Mount Fuji has nothing to compare with this," I murmured. Very gently I stroked her naked back, gradually letting my hands move downward, till at last they rested on the roundness of her buttocks. Immediately I felt a slight tremor of apprehension run through her body. I bent my head and began to kiss her breasts again, and only when I felt the tension dissolve in her muscles did I begin, very tentatively to fondle that delectable bottom. Then suddenly her arms tightened their grip around my back, and she began to cover my face and neck with warm-lipped, passionate kisses.

When she paused for breath I said, "I knew there was wildness among those hills."

"I'm glad you discovered it," she whispered.

We had been standing all this time beside the door, and now I took her by the hand and led her over to the bed. She lay down unbidden, and watched, solemn-eyed, while I took off my dressing gown. Then I went to her and began again with a kiss.

She had some pain, for that was unavoidable; but her wildness wasn't tamed, and it engulfed me in the fiercest, sweetest whirlpool of sensual experience that I had ever known. Afterwards she was very soft and gentle again, and fell asleep with her head pillowed on my shoulder murmuring, "It's a funny thing, but the guilt has all gone away."

I slept more soundly than any night since leaving Japan, and when I opened my eyes the room was filled with morning sunshine. Miranda was curled up beside me, her bottom pressed against my stomach and one of her legs thrust between mine. I raised myself cautiously on one elbow to look at her sleeping face on the pillow. There was the suggestion of a smile on her lips, and the softness of every curving line – cheek, chin, nose, eyelashes and curls – gave it a childlike innocence.

I must have been gazing at her for several minutes when I became aware of a distant roar, rapidly becoming louder. Miranda woke with a start and looked up into my face, just as the noise seemed to be directly overhead. Then there was an ear-shattering explosion that shook the building and blew the tiny panes of glass in the leaded window across the room in a sparkling cascade. Luckily the bed was not in their path.

"It's an air raid!" I shouted, throwing back the bedclothes and leaping out. I searched around for my shoes, calling to Miranda, "Watch out for glass on the floor." I found the shoes and turned my head to see her standing naked at the foot of the bed. Even in that moment of terror the sight of her beautiful body made me catch my breath.

I picked up her raincoat from where it had lain overnight and helped her on with it. "Get your shoes on," I said, struggling into my trousers and grabbing my coat, which had been hanging behind the door. Then I seized my suitcase, which luckily I had not unpacked, and drew back the bolt on the door. "There's bound to be a cellar in this place. Let's get down there." On the landing I stopped to open Bernie's door. He was pulling on his trousers. "What's going on, captain?" he asked.

"It must be an air raid," I replied. "We'd better get down to the cellar." At the foot of the stairs we saw the frightened faces of two of the staff. "Ask them where the cellar is," I said to Bernie.

At that moment we heard the roar of an aircraft engine again. I pulled Miranda to the floor as another explosion shattered out senses. I heard the crash of falling crockery and saw a large iron lantern that was suspended from the ceiling swing like a pendulum on its chain.

I scrambled to my feet. "Let's find that cellar fast," I said. We followed the two servants down a short flight of stone steps into a gloomy cavern. Since there was no light, and none of us had so much as a match, we had to feel our way among the large, wooden casks until we came to a clear space. Sounds from the surface were blotted out.

I laid the suitcase on top of a barrel and said to Miranda, “Feel around in there and you’ll find some clothes. Take some warm things. I’m afraid you won’t be able to match up the colours.” When she had helped herself I fumbled about and found a sweater and two socks – not necessarily a pair – and put them on.

Another explosion shook the roof above our heads. “That one sounded even closer,” said Bernie. A few minutes later there were several lesser, or more distant, impacts.

“I think I’ll go and see what’s happening,” I said. “I can’t imagine what they think their target is.”

Miranda clutched my arm. “Don’t go,” she said.

I drew her close to me and pressed my cheek against hers. “It’s not going to be much of a story if I stay down here,” I said. “I’ve got to see what’s going on. But I won’t be long.” I hugged her tightly, and found her lips with my own.

As I drew away from her she said, “I’m coming with you, then.”

“No. This time you can’t,” I said. As I began to climb I reflected that a few days earlier I would have been going out there without any reluctance, but now I didn’t really want to go. It wasn’t that I wouldn’t have been afraid – I’m as cautious a coward as the next man. But the prospect of a new experience and a dramatic story would have been more important to me than anything else that I could have thought of. Now there was something infinitely more important.

The moment of introspection didn’t last long. I had just stepped out into the passageway when another blast rocked the building. Crouching low, more by instinct than for any good reason, I ran to a shattered window. The opposite side of the square was wreathed in smoke, but I could see that a great chunk had been ripped out of the front of the courthouse and flames were lighting up the exposed interior. Cautiously I put my head through the window and saw another pillar of thick, black smoke swirling into the sky.

Once again I heard the distant growl of a low-flying aircraft, and a moment later I saw it above the housetops – one of the

Typhoons. As it passed out of my line of vision I saw the spurts of flame from the rockets released beneath its belly. The shock of the explosion was a little less violent, and I guessed that the target – if there had been a target – was at the farther end of the town.

For several minutes there was silence, apart from the faint crackle of the flames across the square and the distant sound of voices shouting. I went to the front door, which had been blown inward off its hinges, and cautiously stepped outside. Looking towards the centre of the town I saw people running. Some were carrying bundles, others were leading small children, and they all seemed anxious to get away from their houses. At first the rapidly growing crowd seemed to swirl around in an aimless eddy, but then it changed to a stream, flowing towards the street by which we had entered the town.

As I watched I suddenly became conscious of someone standing beside me. It was Miranda. I couldn't feel anger towards her, but I tried to simulate it, seizing her by the shoulders and saying, "You've no business to be here. Get back in that cellar."

She looked at me calmly, half smiling, and said, "I'm going to stay with you, whatever happens. You can beat me later, for being disobedient."

"That's a very good idea," I said. "Remind me if I forget." And I kissed her fiercely on her eagerly responding lips. Hearing a discreet cough, I looked over her shoulder to see Bernie standing in the doorway, grinning apologetically.

"I'm sorry, captain," he said. "I couldn't hold her. She got away in the dark. Anyhow, it was a bit crowded down there. All the other staff came down, and the dogs. See what I mean?"

"Crowded or not," I said, "this isn't a healthy place to be. They may not have finished yet, and if..." I stopped and listened, hearing the distinctive whirring note of a helicopter.

"Get back inside," I said. "Down on the floor." I ran to the window and crouched behind it, just in time to see a helicopter emerge from the cloud of smoke that hung over the burning courthouse. By its bull-nosed shape it was a Hellcat gunship. As I watched I saw the barrel of its automatic cannon swing downward. There was a flicker of yellow flame at the muzzle as it rattled out a fusillade. The streaks of the tracer shells ripped earthward in the direction of the fleeing crowd, and I heard a rapid series of reports, like the detonation of a giant fire-cracker. The morning air was filled with screams of pain and terror.

The helicopter swung around, following the line of the main street, and fired another short burst as it passed out of sight. I looked behind me and saw that Miranda and Bernie were crouching under a massive oak table. "Stay there," I called out. "I think we've seen the last of the Typhoons, but that helicopter might be back."

As I spoke I heard another helicopter approaching, but looking through the window I could see nothing. The sound increased in volume until it seemed to be directly overhead, and then there was a heavy crash above us, followed by a sharp report. The flickering shadow of the helicopter swept over the sunlit ground outside the window. I looked up and caught a glimpse of two figures at its open doorway, man-handling a gleaming metal cylinder.

"Liquid fire bombs!" I yelled. "Get outside. Bernie, don't let her go. Try and find some cover, but get away from this place."

I ran down the passage that led to the cellar, and flung open the door. "Get out quickly," I shouted. "The inn is on fire." Then realizing that they might not understand Japanese, I repeated the word 'fire' in English. Luckily I remembered it was the same word as the command to shoot, which I had heard many times during the Battle of Stirling.

Then I turned and raced back to the front door. Already ripples of flame were running across the ceilings and dense, black smoke was beginning to billow down the stairs. Outside, I saw Miranda and Bernie running diagonally across the square. She was looking back over her shoulder, and he had her by the arm, half dragging her. I sprinted after them, pausing half-way to look back. The top half of the inn was burning furiously, smoke pouring from the windows and the shattered roof. Several men and women, with two large dogs, were emerging from the smoke-filled doorway. So they had heeded my warning.

I ran on, and saw Bernie pointing towards a roofless cottage, which had been blasted earlier but wasn't burning. He pulled Miranda through the doorway, and seconds later I followed them inside – or rather, behind the wall, for the building was nothing more than a shell containing a heap of rubble.

"They won't bother with this one a second time," said Bernie as I crouched down beside them. Miranda threw her arms around me and pressed her face against my neck.

The second fire bomb had fallen on the wreckage of the courthouse, which now flared up like a miniature volcano. The fleeing crowd had disappeared, but several bodies lay on the roadway.

Looking across the town I caught another glimpse of the helicopter, which must have flown around in a wide arc, and then a cloud of black smoke surged up against the blue sky where it had been. The Hellcat was approaching the square again, and this time we had a clear view as the two crewman swung the bomb out through the doorway, dropping it on a two-storey stone building which had a shop on the ground floor. The bomb crashed through the tiled roof, there was a small explosion and then a tongue of flame licked upward through the hole, followed by an expanding ball of oily, black smoke. In two minutes the building was blazing. The helicopter disappeared from sight.

We crouched in the empty building for about five minutes, straining our ears for the sound of returning aircraft.

"Maybe they've finished their business here," I said at last, standing up. "Let's go and see if we can do anything to help."

We ran to the first of the prostrate bodies, and saw that there was a line of small craters pitting the roadway where the shells had burst. Around them lay the bodies of the victims, four men, six women and three children. Two or three of the bodies were splashed with blood, but most showed no obvious sign of their injuries.

The first was a woman, dressed in black with a grey shawl around her shoulders. I turned her over gently with Bernie's help and saw the jagged hole below her collar bone where a splinter of metal had pierced her chest. A corner of the shawl had been embedded in the wound, blocking the flow of blood, but when we moved her it began to pour out. Even my inexperienced eye could see that she was beyond hope, if not already dead. We moved on to the next, and the next.

Then Miranda called out, "This boy's still alive." We went over to where she was kneeling beside a fair-haired, freckled boy of about ten or eleven whose left arm was badly gashed and bleeding.

"Needs a tourniquet," said Bernie, and ran back to the ruined house to get a piece of wood. Miranda pillowed the boy's head on her lap and comforted him while I went on looking at the other bodies. I found no more alive. Presumably the wounded had been helped away by their companions.

Bernie was applying the tourniquet, and I was on my way back to help him, if I could, when several men appeared, running up the street from the direction in which the crowd had fled. They called out to us and Bernie replied.

"They're asking if we think the planes will come back," he said.

I shook my head. "Tell them that we don't know," I said. "But they'll have to take a chance if they're going to get anybody out alive from the buildings that have been hit."

At first the men seemed uncertain what to do, but then one who was wearing a blue and white brassard appeared and seemed to take command. Several women had also ventured back, and they took the boy, whose bleeding had now been staunched, from Miranda's arms. I noticed that the skirts of her white raincoat were streaked crimson with bloodstains.

The men divided into several groups to search the ruins, for there was obviously no possibility of extinguishing the fires that were still raging. Bernie and I attached ourselves to a group of four who went to the cottage where we had been sheltering, and Miranda followed us, saying, "I don't know much about first aid, but if there's anybody to help I'll do what I can."

We turned over the rubble with our hands and a spade that one of the men had found, but there was no trace of anyone. Possibly they'd got out before the rocket hit the house, but I doubted it. We were just moving away when Bernie pointed to the southern skyline and shouted, "They're coming back!" A black speck against the blue was rapidly taking on the shape of a helicopter.

"Get down and lie still," I yelled. Miranda was lying flat by the time I reached her, and stretched myself on the ground beside her, putting my arm around her shoulders. "They've probably only come back to look at the damage," I said, hugging her tightly.

The helicopter flew directly above us, and by the sound of the engine I thought it wasn't a Hellcat – more likely a Japanese-made

Hawk. In its wake it scattered a snowstorm of small, white leaflets. Bernie put out his hand and caught one as it fell to earth. He read aloud, "Warning. Any person, household, village or town giving shelter or aid to rebels will be instantly and severely punished under the provisions of the Martial Law Declaration. Signed: General Alfred Tettley, British Army Headquarters, Edinburgh Castle."

"So that's what it was – a punitive raid," I said, helping Miranda to her feet. "I should think they've finished with us now."

We went back to helping with the rescue operations, saying little to the grim-faced men who sweated beside us, but feeling the rage that radiated from them. Twelve bodies were uncovered, and six wounded survivors; but there was no doctor in the town, and the treatment that was being dispensed looked fairly primitive to me.

We were resting and drinking some fresh milk that three of the women had brought out in large, earthenware pitchers when Bernie suddenly exclaimed, "The Rough Rider! I wonder what's happened to it." Immediately we ran to the stables, and discovered that, although the roof of the shed had collapsed, shaken by the blasting of a nearby building, the car had suffered only a few bumps and scratches.

We had cleared away the wreckage and were walking back towards the courthouse, where the fire had now almost burnt itself out, when we saw a troop of horsemen coming up the hill at a trot. There were about twenty of them, and as they came closer I could see that they were wearing helmets and uniforms, with blue and white brassards. In the middle of the column I noticed one man who had a red brassard emblazoned with a yellow lotus, to mark his non-combatant medical status. He was leading a pack horse laden with two dark green, canvas panniers.

The troop clattered to a halt and the leader, a tall, lean, golden-bearded man with a youthful, almost boyish, face began talking to the townspeople, who came running from all sides. We joined the edge of the crowd.

"It's Elliot," said Bernie. "They heard the bombing in the Forest and came up to see if they could help." Already the doctor was being led away to the schoolhouse, where the wounded had been taken.

The soldiers dismounted and led their horses down a side street – to put them under cover, no doubt. When they returned they went with some of the townsmen to the courthouse, and began to explore the still smouldering wreckage. Very little remained, except for those parts of the stone walls that hadn't been flattened in the explosions. It seemed that Willie Armstrong and some of his men had been inside when the rockets struck; but the ferocity of the flames had devoured every trace of them.

When the search was ended Elliot walked over to us and said, "My name is Elliot. I hear you came to Selkirk in the hope of meeting me."

"That is so," I replied. "I'm Hashimoto of the *Nagoya Guardian.* I'm glad to meet you, but deeply sorry for the circumstances that have brought you here. This is a terrible thing." He wiped his forehead, leaving dark streaks of soot across the pink skin. "The help you've given has been appreciated," he said. "It was a villainous thing, to bomb a defenceless town and shoot down women and children in the street. They wouldn't dare to come up here and fight us, man to man, but they drop their bombs out of the sky."

I asked if he had seen the leaflets. "If they think they can terrorize the people of Scotland they'll find out what terror really means," was his grim comment.

"But are you not afraid that if your force goes on striking at the English, more towns and villages will suffer the same fate as Selkirk?" I asked.

"Next time the people will be prepared," he answered. "We'll start them digging shelters. And if they burn the houses we can build them up again. But if we lose our freedom, what will our houses be but prisons?"

I asked him about the size of the Striking Force, but he would say only that it was big enough to do its work and small enough to be kept supplied by the people among whom it was based. About its future plans he would, understandably, say nothing.

I commented on the way in which he had been able to evade pursuit, and he replied, "Every man and woman – yes, and every child – in these hills is our eyes and ears. If it wasn't for their aircraft the English would be blind and deaf – and in the night they are."

It was a great pity, I remarked, that Miranda had lost her camera in the destruction of 'The Fleece', for we'd never before had so much need of pictures to help us tell a story. Elliot looked thoughtful for a moment and then turned and shouted to a junior officer, who was giving instructions to a group of townsmen. The young man shouted back a reply, nodding his head.

"Lieutenant Kerr has a camera," said Elliot. "We've found it useful more than once. We travel light and can't carry away with us everything we find on our visits to the enemy. He says there's an unused film in it, so you can take your photographs. The world should see what's being done to Scotland."

So Miranda took her photographs, including several of the troop remounted and ready to return to their secret base. The last picture that she took, before removing the film and giving back the camera to its owner, was published in the *Guardian* about a week later and attracted a great deal of praise. It was a distant shot of the horsemen drawn up in line before the ruined courthouse, and its lack of detail gave it a timeless quality, making it an image of war that could have come from any age.

CHAPTER 8

It was unusual to have snow in London so early in the winter, Miranda told me. However, the flakes that were drifting down through the darkness outside the windows of the Hotel Yedo seemed to be melting as soon as they reached the ground, for I could see no sign of a white carpet beginning to form. Inside it was warm enough, and the tables were well provided with food. War seemed to have brought no austerity to London. Indeed, business appeared to be booming, even though prices were soaring. But I wondered how the people in the shanty towns were managing. Some, of course, must have found work in the army, now swollen by sixty thousand men.

Miranda had gone off for the evening to visit her mother, who lived in the village of Golders Green, somewhere north of the city. Bernie had driven her there in the car, saying that he also had friends in that part of the world. She had asked me to go with her, but I made an excuse that I wanted to be around in case anything important happened during an Assembly debate that evening on the conduct of the war. (Marlowe would be attending it and had promised to let me know if anything dramatic took place.)

Although at the time I wouldn't have admitted it, even to myself, I was afraid that meeting her mother might give our relationship just that promise of permanence I wanted to avoid. It was a childishly carefree, passionate relationship, but I was determined not to lower my last defences and commit myself totally to Miranda. I was too old to make the same mistake a second time, I told myself.

I had allowed myself to be inveigled into dining with Kakuei, the AP reporter I met on the plane from Marseille, and his niece, Haruka, newly arrived from Japan. She was a thin girl, and wore spectacles with frames that slanted upward, emphasizing the sharp triangularity of her face. Her accent and rapidity of speech suggested one of the more fashionable schools for young ladies - possibly Tsuyama College.

Haruka explained that she had come to take up a two-year contract as a teacher of Japanese at the Kanaka Memorial College in London. She had taught abroad once before, with the Overseas

Service Association, in a government school for girls in Antwerp. "A frightfully reactionary establishment," she said. It was a holiday she'd spent in Britain at that time that had made her decide to return when she was qualified.

"It's so much less Easternized here," she declared, "In Antwerp I really felt that our plastic materialism had taken over, but here you can still catch glimpses of the authentic Western way of life. I had thought of going to Ireland, which I've heard is even more unspoilt, but nowadays they don't seem to want expatriate personnel there. Of course, I'm sure they're quite right to keep us out."

"The Irish have retreated back into the mists that the Empire dragged them out of," said Kakuei. "Nobody seems to know what's going on over there now - and I shouldn't think anybody cares."

"Well, I'm certainly going to go and have a look. You can still get tourist visas, can't you?" asked Haruka.

"Oh, no trouble about that," her uncle replied. "There's a lot of coming and going in Dublin these days, with the air-lift to Scotland - though I doubt if most of the people that are running it ever go outside the airport."

"How effective do you think the air-lift's going to be?" I asked him.

"Just enough to prolong the agony for a few more weeks," he said. "I should think the Honanese are hoping they can keep Johnston's army together long enough for the English to get tired of the war and change to a government that will settle with the Scots. But I don't think that' s going to happen. Do you? Since the time that fellow Elliot you got the interview with started taking out villages over the Border I'd say that feeling down here's been hardening; and the raid on Carlisle last night must have killed any chance that Gowrie might have had of winning support for his peace talks proposal."

"I thought the air-lift was to send in food because of the famine," said Haruka,

"That's the part of it you hear most about," said Kakuei, "but my information is that for every plane with food there are three with arms. Anyhow, it all amounts to the same thing in the end. When the guns stop firing or when enough people stop eating the war will be over. But until one or the other happens they'll go on killing and being killed, and all to no purpose. There's nothing humane about helping to prolong that situation. I said as much yesterday to the fellow from the Help Britain Now Fund, and he didn't like it."

"You may be right; but isn't it the opposite of what you were telling that sociology student on the flight from Marseille?" I asked. "You remember - the one who thought famine relief was an imperialist plot?"

Kakuei shook his head, "He wanted to starve people into taking action that would leave them worse off than they were to begin with. All I'm suggesting is that they should be allowed to see the real alternatives - starvation that can't be postponed indefinitely or surrender now and enough to eat."

"But maybe they'd rather die than surrender," Haruka objected.

"Maybe their leaders would rather they died than surrendered," Kakuei corrected her. "For the leaders the alternatives could very well be the opposite way round - except that, if they'd any sense, they'd get on the first plane to Dublin."

"Isn't that the flaw in your argument, though?" I asked. "It would be the people who would suffer if the air-lift was stopped, but they aren't the ones who can take the decision to surrender."

"And wouldn't the government troops massacre them by the thousand if they did?" asked Haruka. "Chancellor Knox has already sent a message to the Union of Peoples, asking for protection under the Convention on Genocide."

"That was a shrewd political move on his part," said her uncle, "but I don't think there's any likelihood of it. I know these fellows can get pretty ferocious when they're worked up, but with the eyes of the whole world on them the British government would take good care to see that it didn't happen."

"If world opinion can force them to keep their soldiers in check, maybe it can force them to make peace," said Haruka. "Don't you think there's a good chance of a resolution at the UP, calling for a truce?" she asked appealing to me.

"I'm afraid I don't think that's very likely," I replied. "Too many governments can see the possibility of something like this happening in their own countries, and they wouldn't want to create a precedent that gave the UP the right to intervene. You try to think of a country that hasn't got a potential minority problem and you'll find yourself hard put to come up with one."

"Well, I think Chancellor Knox might still surprise everybody," said the girl, earnestly. "He sounds like one of those wise old kings in Western legends - Charlemagne or Arthur - who seem to be beaten and then suddenly make some fantastic move that confounds their enemies. Uncle Yutaka says that you've talked to him several times. What do you think of him?"

"He may certainly do something fantastic, but I doubt if it will win him the war. I think he's paranoid."

"Really?" exclaimed Kakuei. "You think he's a nut?"

"Oh, you can't really mean that," said Haruka, "after the way he's held his country together for all these months."

"I could be wrong," I replied, "but I think I've encountered one or two men with his complaint before, and they seem to have a remarkable capacity for winning the loyalty of other people. Maybe there's a bit of the paranoid in most of us, and like calls to like. Or maybe in conflict situations his kind inevitably come to the top. I don't know. But I'm pretty certain that he's as dangerous to his friends as he is to his enemies. And now that he's cornered he'll be as deadly as a cobra, for I'm sure his mind won't accept the reality of what's happening around him."

There was a slight commotion around the dining-room door as a group of new arrivals was ceremoniously ushered in by the head waiter. They were all natives, with the exception of one stout little Japanese in a very expensive suit. A burly, bald-headed man with a fair moustache seemed to be the leader of the party. He was wearing traditional costume, scarlet and white, with a heavy gold chain around his neck.

The party included three of those exquisitely-shaped, expensively-dressed girls, with perfect features and hard, bright eyes, who seem to form an essential part of the decor at a certain kind of social gathering in every country I've visited. They are there, like the flowers and the silverware and the fine ceramics, to provide a visual affirmation of the wealth and importance of the host. And, unlike the other dainties served up to the guests, they are not for consumption;

for they're usually experienced enough to know that the promise of carnal delights can provide them with more profit and less trouble if it remains unfulfilled. As the glittering group was shepherded to its table by an eager gang of waiters Kakuei leaned across towards me and said, "There's the man who's made more out of this war than anybody else - and that's saying something."

"Who is he?" I asked.

"If you didn't spend so much of your time scrambling around in the Scottish mountains you'd know," he replied. "That's the Earl of Lincoln. He's one of the biggest land-owners in the country - has thousands of sheep. And he bought himself a hefty interest in the new woollen industry when the present government decided to sell it off to the private sector last year. Of course, he was a generous subscriber to BPL funds. And by an odd coincidence he got the contract for all the army's new uniforms. I don't think he'll be encouraging anybody to vote for a truce. And there are plenty more like him."

"But isn't there a scandal about it?" asked Haruka.

"Oh, there is - among the people who know the facts. The PDP has been pushing very hard lately, but so far the government has been able to keep a lot of the stink out of the media by saying that things like contracts for army supplies are classified information. I've heard, though, that some of the army boys are starting to get restless, because the goods aren't always up to the mark – rotten meat, leaking boots, mattresses filled with mouldy straw, and all that kind of thing."

Haruka placed her fingertips together and looked very intense. "Do you think corruption is bound to be endemic in developing countries?" she enquired.

"Well, it was endemic in Japan till about a hundred years ago," I replied, "and it still crops up from time to time, even though, I suppose, our record's as good as any in the world. But to avoid it you need well-established procedures for handling public money and a clear acceptance by nearly everybody that public and private interests must be kept separate - and those aren't things you build up over night. I suppose if you shot a few people to encourage virtue in the rest you might get a rapid increase in probity. But then, the condemned man's cousin would probably be in command of the firing-squad, and they'd use blanks."

Haruka laughed - a short, staccato laugh, "It's such a pity that fine old Western traditions like respect for the family seem to make it more difficult to get rid of things like corruption," she said.

"Do you really think it's a fine tradition?" I asked. "I know a little bit about it because we've still got traces of it in the part of Japan where I come from, and I can't say it fills me with any admiration. It's inevitable, of course, when conditions of life are harsh and the social framework is crude, so that individuals have nowhere else but the family to look for protection. But like all protection there's a price to be paid for it. You've only got to look around you here to see what it costs - youth subordinated to age, women to men (with the odd exception), individuality to conformity, strength to weakness, It's the perfect formula for preventing development. I think myself lucky to live in a country where I can pay my taxes and put my trust in Social Security - though I wouldn't mind paying more for a system with fewer gaps in it."

"But what about natural affection?" she objected, "I'm not against pensions and things like that, but I'm sure people are happier being looked after by their own relations than by strangers,"

"And what about the poor, fettered relatives, forced into a role they would never have chosen for themselves and are probably not very good at, anyhow? For that matter, what about the unfortunate victims of their familial care - medical, social, geriatric, psychiatric or whatever? When I broke my arm a couple of years back I was very glad to have a lot of pretty little nurses to look after me, and I wouldn't have swopped them for any selection of aunts or cousins, or daughters if I'd had any."

"Perhaps you're not very strong on natural affection," said Haruka, sharply.

"Maybe I'm not. I happen to think it's a concept that's been carefully fostered by the family as part of its propaganda. Oh, it exists all right, but it's not an inescapable ingredient in every blood relationship. Some parents and children develop loving relationships: others don't, but feel they've got to pretend because of the propaganda. And as for uncles and nephews and cousins and aunts and even brothers and sisters, why in the world should they be expected to feel affection for one another on the sole grounds of a genetic legacy that they happen to share? Why should a woman be condemned to serve as a slave to a father she detests, or a man sacrifice the comforts of his wife and children to bail out some uncle or cousin who's a selfish scoundrel?

"Don't get me wrong," I continued, "I'm not saying that the kind of family system you find in a country like this is totally bad, or even that they could have managed as well up till now if they hadn't had it. What I do say is that changing it will be part of the pricc they'll have to pay if they want a state of affairs where everybody can be certain of two square meals a day, and can see his children having some choice of jobs to work at and a chance to live for more than forty years."

"Yes, and along with those benefits I suppose they'll have to accept our plastic materialism. That's what worries me," said Haruka.

"Is it that much worse than the materialism of mud and manure that it'll replace?" I asked, "I suppose we've substituted the hypocrisy of public relations for the cant of religion, but that's about the only difference,"

"You're very cynical," she said, disapprovingly.

"That's not cynicism," her uncle interjected. "That's the armour that newspapermen wear to protect them from the poisoned arrows of disillusionment. The ones that haven't got it need drugs like alcohol and hashish to heal the wounds."

By this time we had finished the meal and were indulging in that very civilized Middle Western custom of coffee-drinking, which has now spread even to places like London. I was pouring Haruka a second cup when I saw Marlowe standing in the doorway, snowflakes in his hair and an excited expression on his face. He strode towards us calling out "It's unbelievable. You should have been there."

"What's happened?" I asked. "Has the government been defeated?"

"Quite the opposite," he replied, sitting down. "The government has got rid of the Assembly."

"Got rid of it!" Kakuei exclaimed. "What do you mean."

Although Marlowe was clearly upset by his own news, he couldn't resist smiling with the satisfaction that a bearer of bad tidings derives from the suspense of his hearers.

"When Serjeant had won the first vote he promptly introduced a bill suspending the Assembly, and all political activity, for the duration of the war. There's to be a Council of State to pass legislation."

"Who'll be on that?" asked Kakuei.

"It's just the government plus a couple of generals and two tame 'representatives' of Scotland and Wales."

"Not Enoch Ap Hwyel?" asked Kakuei with a chuckle. (Ap Hwyel was a Welsh member of the Christian Heritage Party in the Assembly who had reacted strongly against the government's savage repression of the September riots in Caernarfon, and had set up his own party. It called for a federal system, under which Wales would have a large measure of autonomy, including the right to expel anyone who didn't have at least three Welsh grandparents.)

"Far from it," Marlowe replied. "His Plaid Cymru Party hasn't just been suspended, like the People's Democratic Party. It's been made illegal."

"Well, that's pretty stupid, even from the government's point of view," I said. "Ap Hwyel had diverted the Welsh firebrands into harmless political activities. Now they'll probably take to their mountains and start throwing rocks at anybody who goes near them."

"They've not got much else to throw" said Kakuei, "I wasted a week trailing round their sodden valleys and I didn't see a single gun."

"What reasons did Serjeant give for shutting down the Assembly?" I enquired.

"The usual stuff that you get when a one-party state is in the making," Marlowe answered gloomily. "The nation couldn't afford the luxury of opposition when it was fighting for its existence. And all the defeatist talk about negotiations with the rebels was undermining the morale of the armed forces - there could be no talks with treason."

"But I thought some of his own boys were a bit critical about the conduct of the war," Kakuei interjected.

Marlowe nodded several times. "Yes, but he had a juicy bone

to throw to them. Elliot's Raiders were rounded up and destroyed this afternoon."

"How did it happen?" I asked, the image of a boyish face with a golden beard flashing through my mind.

"They over-reached themselves by going for Carlisle, I suppose," he replied. "The local volunteer force put up a good fight, and there was a company of regular infantry to strengthen them, so the Raiders got tied up in a street battle all through the night, and weren't able to disengage till nearly dawn. And then a helicopter spotted the horses' tracks in the snow, somewhere in Eskdale, and the gunships cut them off at Davington before they could get under cover. According to the army not many escaped, but the paras are still deployed in force around the foot of Ettrick Pen."

"What about Elliot himself?" I asked.

"He hasn't been identified among the dead or the prisoners."

"So the Members think the war can be won, now that audacious O'Neill has replaced the bungling Tettley?" asked Kakuei. "Did you know O'Neill is Irish, by birth? I wonder what Ap Hwyel would make of that, if he was still interested."

"The important thing for you," said Marlowe, standing up, "is that Gowrie, the leader of the PDP, is giving a Press conference at the Assembly tonight, before they finish the second reading of the bill. Serjeant is rushing it through, but until it' s been voted on the second time it won't have the force of law and the PDP is still free to say what it pleases. Are you coming?"

Kakuei and I were both on our feet in an instant, making our apologies to Haruka. We took a taxi through the snowy streets to the Assembly and found a dozen other reporters arriving on the same errand as ourselves. The conference was being held in the Oval Committee Room, and I admired the modern pine panelling as we waited for Gowrie to arrive. The building had been designed by the famous Japanese architect, Suzuki, Marlowe told me.

Gowrie came straight from the Chamber, where the debate was still going on. I had seen him only once before, and so couldn't make any real comparisons, but I thought that, in spite of his youth, he looked tired and dejected. His shoulders were hunched and his head was bent forward, a lock of wavy hair flopping over his forehead.

He started by outlining what had happened in the Assembly that evening. Every now and then he tilted back his head and thrust out his chin, as though defying fate to do its worst. The system of democratic government, established amid all the difficulties and dangers of independence, was now under the shadow of extinction, he declared.

"Let no one be under any illusion about what is meant by the term 'suspension', "he went on. "It is merely the first step on the downward path that leads to dictatorship."

And what had been the reasons given for this action, he asked. To unite the country in the face of danger - but nothing could be more divisive than what the government was now doing. He continued: "Mr. Serjeant says that he will not talk with treason. No one wants him to talk with treason. What I've said - and I'll say it again - is that total military victory can be gained only at the cost of destroying, perhaps for ever, the hope of re-uniting this island as one people with a sense of common destiny. Let us be prepared, then, to talk to anyone - and I repeat, anyone - who is ready to repent of treason and work for an end to the killing of brother by brother.

“How many more of our young men - Englishmen and Scotsmen and Welshmen, all of them British - must redden the winter snow with their blood, and how much more of our treasure, that should be used for educating them in the arts of peace and providing constructive work for them to do, must be burned up in bombs and bullets?" In spite of the high-flown politician's phrases, he sounded sincere.

"And there are other questions that we have been asking, questions that may explain this government's eagerness to silence those voices that have the constitutional right - indeed the duty - to interrogate it on its conduct of the nation’s business," he went on. "Who are the men who have profited so hugely from this country's misfortunes? What are their relationships with the British People's League? How have they carried out the contracts so lavishly bestowed on them? How many members of the government have interests in business enterprises supplying the armies in the field?

“What promises have been made to foreign governments and companies in return for the vast inpouring of money and material consumed in this unnecessary war?” he went on. “How much of our children's future have we already mortgaged to pay for one man's stubborn refusal to sit down around a table and talk?" He paused and passed a blue handkerchief over his perspiring brow.

The speech ended with a plea to the media to tell the world what was being done to democracy in Britain. "Take a copy of what Mr. Serjeant has said tonight, with all his promises to preserve the rule of law and to restore the democratic process as soon as hostilities have ended," Gowrie advised his hearers, "and stick it on the wall above your typewriter. And every time he keeps a promise, or every time he breaks one, tick it off. At least he'll know there's somebody watching him who still has a voice that he can't muzzle. For I trust that those of you who come from countries overseas will continue to enjoy the freedom in your writing of which we used to boast, but which now has been snatched away from us in the name of national security."

He would say little in answer to questions about his own future, except that he intended to remain in readiness to serve the country. Exactly how much public activity would be permitted to himself and his colleagues under the new law he thought it impossible to predict; but he said he had confidence in the judiciary to interpret it in ways that would not make a mockery of the freedoms guaranteed under the Constitution.

Then it was time for him to return to the Chamber. The vote was expected within the hour. At the door he turned, his face pale and his chin thrust out, and said in his slow and careful Japanese, "Gentlemen, this could be the last vote that is taken in the British Assembly in our lifetime."

Marlowe turned to me, looking more serious than I had ever seen him before. "You don't realize how much freedom means to you until you've lost it," he said.

We waited in the building until the inevitable result had been announced. Then we went out into the darkened street, where the snow had stopped falling, but the slush squelched dismally under our feet as we searched for a taxi in the biting wind.

CHAPTER 9

There was a moment of muscle-tautening tension as the wheels of the Mitsubishi Hiroshima 107 made contact with the runway at Aberdeen. The four mighty engines emitted a deafening roar as the brakes were applied and we bounced and skidded for several seconds that seemed like minutes; but then I felt the aircraft come under control and the speed begin to slacken. I looked at the faces of my three companions in the cramped space that had been left clear for passengers. One of the two Honanese, an ex-paratrooper by his own account, was calmly chewing gum, but the other, who had also come to ply the trade of a mercenary, was yawning with relief. I guessed that the third man, a young Japanese from Kyushu, was thinking about his rabbits.

I had seen the two crates containing rabbits being loaded into the plane at Dublin, and on hearing my exclamation of surprise Jutaka Shigenbo had introduced himself and enthusiastically explained their purpose. He was working for the Help Britain Now Fund and had been behind the lines in Scotland twice before, he told me, organizing food distribution. One of the things that was now urgently needed was more protein, for most of the available livestock had long since been slaughtered and eaten, partly because of a lack of fodder to keep it alive. So he had hit on the idea of rabbits - "easy to feed and quick to breed"; and the crates contained what he hoped would be the progenitors of a long line of soups and stews. And the skins would make a modest contribution to keeping the cold out of children's heads and feet.

During the flight Jutaka told me that before the war and the setting up of the Fund he had been working for the Whole Earth Alliance, a small, Japanese-based voluntary organization, on a development project in a remote area in eastern Britain called Lincolnshire. From his description it sounded incredibly primitive, bounded on the seaward side by a region of wild and desolate marshland, where people lived by hunting and fishing in much the same way as they had for hundreds of years. He had been working among a farming community a little way inland, where the soil was good for agriculture. The main problem, he said, was that so much of the arable land had been turned over to sheep farming by the local landowner, the Earl of Lincoln, that the peasants hadn't enough space on which to support their growing numbers.

When I asked why the government, which had been pledged to land reform, hadn't done anything about this situation, Jutaka said he supposed it was because wool was an important export that earned a lot of badly-needed foreign exchange. He had been working with a locally-organized peasants' co-operative, founded by a schoolmaster called Hereward Townsend. The main aim was to help the peasants buy their supplies of seeds and fertilizers and so on without going through middlemen who took an exorbitant profit, and without having to borrow from moneylenders who charged fifty per cent interest, or more.

The scheme had been working well, Jutaka said, although it had been handicapped by the lack of people who could write and read and do simple accounts. But he had been helping out there, and teaching some of the peasants at the same time. All sorts of other activities had been springing up around the co-operative. They had introduced new crops to supplement the very limited staple diet of bread, root vegetables, eggs and a little pork and fish when they were available - and ale, of course.

Beans had been an important innovation, he explained, both because they provided protein that people were short of and because they helped to nourish the soil. And the peasants had never seen potatoes before, but now they were finding them a great stand-by in hard times, for both people and pigs. There were classes in nutrition and hygiene, too, for the women; and a scheme to sell surplus vegetables in Nottingham and Peterborough had just been started.

When the project had been getting under way, Jutaka told me, some of the Earl of Lincoln's bully-boys had tried to break it up. There had been threats to Townsend and to some of the peasants, and a communally-owned pair of horses had been hamstrung in their stable one night. But the local BPL Assembly member had taken an interest and used his influence to get some police activity in the neighbourhood, and so the trouble had died down.

Jutaka had been reluctant to leave the Lincolnshire project, but had nevertheless volunteered for secondment to the Help Britain Now Fund when the opportunity arose. "I could speak the language - at least to half of them," he said. He thought there would be a quarter of a million deaths in Scotland before the end of the winter if the blockade wasn't lifted.

When the plane came to a halt on the floodlit runway Jutaka immediately went off to see to the unloading of his rabbits. The two mercenaries had other cargo to attend to. I suddenly felt lonely - on all my other expeditions in this war Bernie and Miranda had been with me, but now I'd had to leave them behind. There had been only one place on the overloaded plane. And I'd also thought that a period of separation from Miranda might help to keep the relationship under control.

Suddenly an army scout car drove into the floodlit area and drew up beside me. A short, dark young officer stepped out and said: "You are Mr. Hashimoto?" I confirmed that I was.

"General Mackie has sent me to meet you," he said. "I am Lieutenant McSkimming. The General sends you his greetings and looks forward to seeing you tomorrow."

And so I spent the remainder of that night in a large building - a school, I think - in Aberdeen that had been taken over by the army, and on the following morning set out in the company of McSkimming for Perth. He was a taciturn young man, but gradually I persuaded him to talk. Mackie had been a general for a fortnight, I discovered, and McSkimming was his aide-de-camp. The young man had been promoted immediately after the Battle of Gleneagles, which had stabilized the new defence line in the Ochil Hills.

Once he began to talk more freely I discovered that that line was going to be much more difficult to hold than the long-defended positions on the Forth, from which the Scots had finally been blasted. The length of the new front presented a manpower problem, and there were great difficulties in keeping open good communications between various units, although the terrain did afford some advantages to the defence. But it was clear, he indiscreetly confided to me, that Johnston wanted to abandon Perth and pull the defence line back quite a long way, probably as far as Brechin. Knox and Mackie took a very different view, I gathered.

We drove into Perth, a place much changed from the tranquil town that I remembered from that autumnal morning. Bomb-shattered and fire-blackened buildings were much in evidence, and there was a beleaguered feeling about the deserted streets. Only in the centre did I see a flash of colour. The guard was being changed at the heavily sand-bagged town hall - or the 'Chancellery', as McSkimming described it. With their trousers made of tartan cloth, white tunics and burnished steel helmets the guardsmen swaggered in splendour against their drab backcloth.

In the gloomy, marble grandeur of the entrance hall I was met by General Mackie, resplendent also in a white tunic, with a broad, blue sash around the waist. He greeted me cordially, and told me I had arrived just in time to accompany the Chancellor on a tour of the refugee camp. Some local reporters, two other foreigners and a Honanese television crew would be coming as well. We all set off a quarter of an hour later in a little cavalcade of vehicles, the Chancellor's car escorted by four cavalrymen in white tunics riding lean grey horses.

I was astonished to see how the refugee camp that I visited three months before had increased in size. It now covered something like ten times the area. We were driven straight to the centre where several large wooden buildings had been erected to house the administration and a small hospital. Knox descended from his car and was greeted by the camp officials while the television camera whirred. Among the welcoming party I noticed my old acquaintance, Osamu the monk, who acknowledged my presence with his eyebrows when he caught sight of me.

The formalities over, Knox made a brisk inspection of the central buildings, slowing down in the hospital to speak to some of the emaciated patients. There was a fetid atmosphere in the long, low building, the floor of which was crammed with mattresses, and I was glad to get back into the frosty air outside, tainted though it was with the odours of too many people living too close to one another. We were next conducted to a nearby section of the camp to meet some of the refugees. I noticed that this particular warren of makeshift huts showed signs of having been tidied up. The pathways had been swept, the aluminium buckets had been polished up, some of the huts had new timber or corrugated iron in them, and all the people who were brought out to meet the Chancellor had been thoroughly washed. But nothing could disguise their hunger and the perpetual cold that was in their inadequately protected bones. Gaunt, sunken cheeks and shivering, stick-like limbs were all around us, and the swollen bellies of the children were bursting through their rags.

At first the refugees were quiet and subdued, answering deferentially the questions that Knox addressed to them. But then one or two of the men began to question him and the crowd began pressing closer to hear his answers.

"What are they saying?" I asked McSkimming, who was standing beside me.

He looked worried. "They want to know when the food is coming," he said. "There was no delivery to the camp yesterday, it seems. They're asking where the food from the air-lift has gone."

More voices were raised now, shrilly and hoarsely, and I saw Knox raise both hands in a placatory gesture. Then he turned and began to move hurriedly back in the direction from which we had come. The crowd was now swelling rapidly and pressing in on the party of visitors from all sides. I was jostled and swept along until I suddenly found myself alongside the great bulk of the Chancellor.

I had turned my head to look up at his bright red, sweat-covered face when, out of the corner of my eye, I saw a large object hurtling through the air in my direction. Instinctively I raised my arm to protect my head. The object, a rough log about a metre in length, struck my forearm and was deflected to the ground - or on to the toes of some of the crowd.

At that moment two of the cavalry escort came cantering towards us, clearing a path with the butts of their lances. My arm felt numb and I noticed that my sleeve was torn and blood was seeping through the gash, where a projecting stump must have ripped the material. The crowd had begun to melt away at the first sight of the cavalrymen, and I found myself surrounded by solicitous officials. I was about to make light of the incident when I realized that they thought I had protected Knox from the missile, Possibly I had, although that hadn't been my intention.

Mackie took my arm, to look at the wound. Then Knox, who seemed to have been speechless with emotion, addressed me, "Scotland is indebted to you, young man. This time, as well as showing your ability to be on the spot when the news is being made, you've helped to make it."

He extended a podgy hand and patted my shoulder. Then he exclaimed: "Aha! I see an angel of mercy who will look to your wound."

I followed the direction of his gaze and saw the white-uniformed figure of a nurse standing on the steps of a long, low, wooden building a little way ahead of us. We moved towards her, and Knox called out in Japanese, "Young lady, we have a casualty for you." I saw then that the girl had an Eastern face.

It was an attractive face, almost beautiful, with a fine bone structure and a very light complexion. The mouth was small and full-lipped and the eyes, behind horn-rimmed spectacles, were large and lustrous. The girl was short and rather stockily built, but with a fullness around the top of her white overall that suggested a splendid bosom underneath the stiff, unflattering fabric.

She opened the door behind her and led us into the building, which I saw at once was some kind of children's hospital unit. A space near the door had been separated from the rest by curtains to serve as an office and store-room, and as the nurse led me in there I saw that the rest of the building was crowded with little bodies, some lying still under blankets, others sitting listlessly, a few moving around. A fair-haired nurse was in the centre, near the huge iron stove, bathing a naked girl in an aluminium tub.

"Take off your jacket and let's have a look," the girl said briskly, helping me out of my fleece-lined windcheater. Gently she unbuttoned the shirt sleeve and folded it back. The bleeding had stopped now and she began swabbing away the drying blood with cotton wool dipped in some kind of antiseptic solution. I winced slightly and she said mockingly, "Don't be a baby. It's not much more than a scratch."

"I know," I said. "I feel a bit of a fraud, taking up your time. The babies out there," I nodded my head towards the curtain, "need your attentions much more than I do."

"Oh, it makes a change," she said, starting to bandage the wound. "You've got a nasty bruise there, too, I'm afraid."

I asked her how many children were in the hospital and she told me about fifty. Besides herself there was another Japanese-trained nurse and three untrained Scottish girls. The doctor from the main hospital block supervised their work. All the patients were affected by lack of food, she said, and for more than half of them proper food was the only cure that would have any effect. "But we just don't have enough," she added, pushing up my shirt sleeve to give me an anti-tetanus injection.

As she was helping me into my jacket she said, "If you'd like that tear sewn up and you're still around this evening, I'll do it for you when I go off duty."

"That's very kind of you," I replied. "Where will I find you?"

"I'm billetted at 'The Salutation.' Do you know where it is?"

I nodded. "It's good to get away from this place for a few hours," she said. "I go off at six o'clock. If you like to look me up about seven I'll have sorted myself out, and I should still be awake."

"I'll be there," I said. "By the way, what's your name?"

"Hiroko Masao," she replied.

We went out from behind the curtain and saw Knox and several of his staff talking to the Scots nurse and looking at some of the children. Knox was mopping his eyes with a large, red handkerchief. As we approached he blew his nose loudly.

"It's tragic, young man," he said in a strangulated voice. "These unfortunate little souls, every one of them precious in the sight of our Lord and His Holy Mother - their little bodies are ravaged through the wickedness of evil men. Look at them," he said, bending his huge bulk to pick up a shrivelled, red-haired little boy whose huge blue eyes stared out from the ash-white face of an old man, "and ask yourself, 'If John Serjeant could see them would he still send his ships and his planes to stop their food from reaching them?' But he has seen them, has he not - in those excellent photographs taken by that talented young woman who accompanied you on your last visit? Then, of course, conditions were very much better than the terrible scene that you see before you today."

Emboldened by the favour I seemed to be enjoying, I commented, "On that occasion you seemed confident that food supplies would last the winter, Chancellor. What has happened to alter the situation?"

He looked at me intently and nodded his head slowly, several times. "You are asking a very important question, young man. I remember something that was said to me once by my father, who was a very wise man, though he lived all his life humbly and without taking any great part in public affairs. He said, 'If you can trust the men who ride behind you, you need have no fear when you charge the enemy.' Do you follow my meaning?"

Without pausing for an answer he turned to Mackie and said, "My heart is torn for all of Scotland's children but especially for these little ones, here present. There is little we can do at this moment, but let us do what we can. I want every last morsel of food in the Chancellery kitchen to be put in a truck and brought here to give strength and nourishment to these children. They are the future of Scotland, not us. Will you see that it is done, General Mackie?"

Mackie saluted and turned to McSkimming. I couldn't understand what he said, but recognized the word 'television'. Then McSkimming saluted and hurried away.

"You will be able to save some of the food for Christmas, nurse," Knox said, turning to Hiroko, who was smiling delightedly.

She looked a little puzzled, but replied, "Oh, yes. Yes, of course. Thank you for your wonderful generosity. It'll make so much difference to the children. All they need is more food - most of them."

He beamed benevolently and patted her shoulder with a podgy hand. "And is your larger patient fit to travel?" he asked.

"Oh, yes. He'll be all right now," she replied, giving me a sidelong glance.

"Then he must come with me and have some lunch." He turned to Mackie again. "We'll eat at headquarters, since there'll be nothing left in the Chancellery."

As we were trooping out of the building with the wails of a dozen unhappy children ringing in our ears, Hiroko, who was standing by the door, said to me, "See you this evening, then."

Now that the front had moved back, northward, the army's headquarters had been set up just outside Perth. A large, solidly-built, stone farmhouse which, with its outbuildings, enclosed a square courtyard, had been chosen for the purpose. It was sheltered on three sides by a grove of pine trees, and a lot of care had been taken to preserve its agricultural appearance. The dunghill was intact, chickens still ran around the courtyard, and the vehicles parked under the trees were covered with camouflage nets.

Knox, Mackie, three junior officers and I sat down to lunch at a long table, waited on by two orderlies. Although the meal was fairly frugal, everyone seemed to treat it as a sort of regal occasion. Knox placed me at his right hand, apparently as a mark of honour, and gradually became quite expansive towards me.

"Young man," he said, ladling himself out a second helping of stew, "I have spent a great deal of my life pondering the human condition. When I was a boy I suffered from illness, and consequently I spent a lot of time in the solitude of my own room. It was then that I had the leisure to reflect on the strange behaviour of my elders, and to wonder if I might not be able to do better than they had done if I were given the chance. Little did I think then that one day it would fall to me to lead our beloved country."

He paused and looked severely at Mackie. "General Mackie," he said, "you have left two carrots. In these times, when so many are starving, we must set a personal example by not allowing so much as a morsel of food to go to waste."

Shamefacedly the General began to eat his carrots.

Knox swallowed a few more mouthfuls of stew and resumed his address to me, "I have always believed that justice must prevail, even though great patience may be needed to secure it. I remember when I was at school there was a youth called Douglas in my class who was big for his age. He was a bully and he terrorized the school. More than once I suffered at his hands, but I was patient and showed no resentment. Then, one day, one of the masters lost his gold watch; and when a search was made the watch was found in Douglas's desk. He protested his innocence but the evidence was against him, and he was flogged and expelled from the school. Only I knew how that watch had got there - but I also knew that justice had been done." The officers roared with appreciative laughter.

A large, circular cheese was placed on the table, and as everyone cut themselves chunks from it I tried to probe a little into what the Chancellor really thought about the military situation. "Winter is our strongest ally," he proclaimed. "We had some snow a few days ago and the English didn't know where to put themselves. It'll be back again before long, and then there'll be some changes. Our men are hardened, and they're fighting in the hills now, where they know the lie of the land and the enemy doesn't."

"But won't the cold weather make the food shortage more

acutely felt?" I asked.

"Young man," he said, beaming at me, "your heart is sound. You feel for the sufferings of Scotland. And what you say is partly correct, but only partly. For a few days, or maybe even a week, the hardships will be increased. But then, when the enemy has been rolled back, we shall regain possession of the storehouses of Falkirk and Glasgow and Edinburgh, and the load of hunger will be lifted from the shoulders of our people. We must endure to conquer, and some must suffer. Alas, that it should so often be the smallest and the weakest."

A tear ran along the rim of his spectacles and trickled down his plump cheek. He fumbled in his pocket and produced a large, red handkerchief, saying, "I can't put out of my mind those poor children, with their tiny, wasted limbs. They are the sacrifice that's being made for Scotland." He removed his spectacles and mopped his eyes. "And yet, we must take comfort from the thought that Almighty God had to sacrifice his only-begotten son to save the world from sin. Why should we expect to be more favoured in what is demanded of us?"

I asked whether he thought the changed political situation in London was to Scotland's advantage or disadvantage, and he brightened immediately. "Aha! You have reminded me of what I was about to say a little earlier," he replied. "Scotland has a second ally in the disunity of the English themselves. Serjeant has taken it upon himself to rule without the consent of the people. He can do that only if victory sits upon his shoulder. When his army has once again been routed he'll be exposed for what he is - a man who promises a great deal, but can deliver nothing. Then we'll see how long the English will to fight can last."

While my favoured position held I thought I would exploit it a little further, so I asked: "Have you no doubts, then, about the will to fight among any of your own people?" Knox's face immediately became very serious, and I saw him glance at Mackie.

"I trust you, young man, and therefore I'll be frank with you," he said. "There have been a few - a very few, who have talked faint-heartedly of trying to negotiate a truce with the invader while half of Scotland still lies bleeding under his heel. I can only guess at their reasons. They may have been bought with gifts or promises. Or it may be that, lacking the benefit of a Christian upbringing, they don't share the full measure of Scottish manhood, and cannot understand that, although Almighty God may chasten his people, he will give them the final victory."

He removed his glasses and smiled at me benignly. "You know, young man, there are times when I am up there," he said, pointing his fat forefinger at the ceiling, "looking down on Andrew Knox, struggling to make the right decision. And then I think how simple life would be if only we would live it by those great, eternal truths preserved for us by our Holy Mother Church - as I have always tried to do. Truth cannot lie down with falsehood. Those who are not for us are against us, and we deceive ourselves if we think otherwise."

He seemed to forget my presence and turned towards Mackie with an almost frightened look in his watery eyes. "There are certain things to be done, General Mackie, and it would be better if they were to be done quickly. Find out if one of the foreigners understands the work - it would be better that way. We will be generous to a good workman."

Mackie raised his dark eyebrows inquiringly and Knox made a peremptory gesture with his thumb towards the door. "Now," he said. "There is no time like the present; and these arrangements can't be hurried."

Then he turned to me. "You will forgive us, I know, young man, but matters of state are pressing. The problems of every man in Scotland come to rest on these unworthy shoulders. But God supplies the strength we need."

He rested his palms on the table, which creaked as he heaved up his huge frame. "Take good care of that arm - it's an honourable wound. And keep in touch with General Mackie. We may yet have something to show you as worthy of your pen as that first expedition on which you accompanied us. Blessings on you." He raised his hand in a gesture of benediction and moved towards the door, which the three officers rushed to open for him.

I walked briskly back to the town, glad to be out in the cold, winter sunlight.

CHAPTER 10

The candlelight behind her produced a kind of halo around Hiroko's head as she opened her door to me. (There was no longer any electricity in Perth.) She was wearing a long robe of dark crimson silk embroidered with gold that flattered her stocky figure and concealed the sturdy calves and ankles I had seen beneath her nurse's uniform. Its low neckline gave a glimpse of breasts unusually well developed for an Eastern girl. Her skin was very pale and, now that she had removed her glasses, her almond eyes were arresting. They were set in a heart-shaped face with a crown of soft, glossy black hair, cut short and curving inward and upward around the top of her jaw. Her small, neat mouth revealed a line of faultless teeth as she smiled at me.

"Come in," she said. "It's a tiny little room, but I'm lucky to have it - and the bed is comfortable. I would hate to have to sleep down in the camp. Apart from anything else, the smell is so awful."

"I wondered if you got used to it," I said, closing the door behind me. She gestured to me to sit in the only chair, while she perched on the side of the high bed.

"You don't notice while you're working; but I've found that when I come off duty and step outside the hospital it seems to start closing in on me."

"How long have you been here?" I asked.

"Since the beginning of last month. I was in Aberdeen before that, in a clinic and day nursery for the children of women who work in the fish market. I'm with World Children's Welfare. Then they sent me down here with Mariko, the other nurse, to open a children's hospital in the camp."

"That can't have been an easy job," I said.

"Oh, the WCW Field director helped us to get it going, and that was the easiest part. It started getting worse when we realized we weren't going to be able to cure any of them unless we could get more food. We can make them a bit more comfortable, get rid of some of their pains, but we can't put strength back into them. They die like the leaves on the trees. Let's have that jacket of yours."

I took it off, and was glad of the log fire burning in the grate.

"It's very kind of you to do it, after a hard day's work," I said. "I usually carry a needle and thread myself, but on the flight in here I had to travel even lighter than usual."

"That's all right," she said, smiling. "I wouldn't have offered, only I wanted somebody to talk to. You've no idea how lonely it can be, even with thousands of people all round you. I only see Mariko for a few minutes when we take over duty from one another. The Scottish girls are all right, but they don't talk much Japanese."

She opened the heavy dressing-table and brought out a little satchel containing sewing equipment. "It's like being trapped, and I sometimes wonder if I'll ever get out again. What's really happening in the war?" From a deep pocket in the crimson robe she produced her glasses and put them on, thereby seeming to bring the soft lines of her face into a sharply angular focus.

"I'd say it's only a matter of time - how much time probably depends on whether Johnston can bring off another of those brilliant tactical moves that he's so good at," I replied. "If the government forces have another setback it might shake their confidence and make them less willing to move in for the kill. But that'll mean another couple of months of slow starvation for the Scots. Of course, somebody might get through the blockade with a few big shipments. The British Navy hasn't enough patrol boats to watch all the ports on the west coast and up in the north. But if the food was landed I don't know how they'd get it across here, through the mountains, with scarcely any transport. And anyhow, I don't think even the Honanese have enough faith now in Knox's ability to win for them to consider the effort worthwhile."

"I could never understand why they gave him so much help in the first place," said Hiroko, biting off the thread with her neat little teeth.

"Well, the oil concessions could be worth a great deal, and Serjeant had already committed himself to us and the Shantungese; so it was their only hope of getting in on a very profitable act. And of course, you know what the Honanese President, Ta-shih is like. Once he gets an idea he thinks he's been inspired by heaven and nothing will make him change his mind. Indeed, he reminds me a little of Knox, though I think he's just a bit saner."

She arched her sharply-defined eyebrows in surprise. "You

think Knox isn't... sane?"

"I wouldn't say that he's certifiable, but definitely a little bit paranoid. Don't you think so?"

"Today was the first time I'd seen him close to," she replied. "I thought he was rather sweet. A bit peculiar, maybe - but then, these people are more emotional than we are. By the way, what did he mean about saving some of the food for something or other? I can't remember the word."

"For Christmas. It's a Christian festival when they celebrate the birth of one of their gods - or their god in one of his manifestations, I should say. I think they have a lot of feasting and give each other gifts a bit like our Fizo Bon." I remembered that Miranda had promised to have a party if I was back in time.

"Oh, I must remember that," she said, her eyes brightening. "We can try to give the children some kind of treat. I expect it'll be the last that most of them will ever have. When is it?"

I searched my memory for what Miranda had said. "I think it's in six days' time. But your Scots girls will know."

"Oh, of course they will," she exclaimed. "Anyhow, I'm jolly grateful to Chancellor Knox for his extra food, even though most of it wasn't really suitable."

"What was the matter with it?" I asked.

"There were all kinds of things the children couldn't digest. Lots of tinned stuff and pickles and bottled sauces. But we swapped them with the camp kitchen for more porridge meal and powdered milk. I don't see anything mad about being generous on an impulse."

"Nor do I. And what he did may even have been impulsive, though I'm not certain about that," I said. "But my judgment is based on a slightly longer acquaintance with him. I've seen the victims of some of his other bright ideas."

She shrugged, her shoulders. "I expect you're right, then," she said, holding up the sleeve to see if it needed any more stitches. "I don't know much about mental illnesses - though I've been to a psychotherapist myself. That was an interesting experience."

"Really?" I said, in some surprise, looking at her calm self-assured little face. "Can I ask what the trouble was?"

"Oh, I had a sort of breakdown. Trouble in love - you know." She smiled wryly. And then the thought struck me that the brisk, matter-of-factness of her speech was .just a shade too rapid to be natural.

"Did that have anything to do with your decision to come and work out here?" I asked.

Her eyebrows shot up again. "Yes, as a matter of fact, it did. How did you guess that?"

"Well, something a little bit similar happened to me once," I replied. "But that was a long time ago. Any special reason for choosing Britain?"

"Yes. My father was here in the army - a long time ago. He used to tell me stories about it when I was little, and he'd brought back a lot of carvings and pictures and stuff. I don't usually do things for sentimental reasons, but I was in the mood at that particular time, I suppose. That's one mistake I'll never repeat."

"You're sorry that you came here?" I asked.

"Wouldn't you be, if you were me? Oh, I liked it at first in Aberdeen. When you're feeling that nobody loves you there's nothing quite as good as children. They show every little bit of affection that they feel, and being with them is like bathing in a warm pool - not that they couldn't be little devils sometimes. And I felt I was needed, which was important for me, too.

"But after the novelty had worn off the loneliness started. There was absolutely nothing to do up there, and only four other Japanese people within a hundred miles. I suppose I should have tried to mix a bit more with the natives but they're… well, a bit primitive, really. The educated one's aren't so bad, though there aren't many of them.

"But I soon found out it wasn't safe to be alone with one of the men. Their religion is very queer about sex, you know. They're all so repressed, and they seem to think a single foreign woman who wears short skirts and trousers must be available for the asking. It's a pity I didn't fancy any of them. Mind you, I had four offers of marriage, and I think two of them were serious." She smiled and bit off the end of the thread to finish the sewing.

"And then you came down here, I suppose." I said.

"Yes. I wanted to come. It seemed a chance to do something that was really desperately needed, and in a way it was. But without enough food it's hopeless. If I could see just some of them getting better I wouldn't mind being cut off in this place, and working so long that I sometimes feel my legs won't carry me another step. But I come back here when I'm off duty and wonder what's the point of it all. You know, the first time a baby died I couldn't stop crying for half an hour. Now I feel hardly anything when it happens - except the sort of ache that I have all the time when I look at them. It frightens me, the way I've changed."

She stuck the needle back in its case and handed me the jacket. "You'd better put it on," she said. "The evening seems to be getting chillier." And she went over to the fireplace to add another log to the fire. I stood up and put the jacket on.

Hiroko was returning to her seat on the bed when the thud of a nearby explosion - not a very heavy one - rattled the casement. She flung her arms around me and pressed her face against my chest, exclaiming: "Oh, no! I can't stand it any more. It's another air raid."

I could feel her whole body trembling as I put my hands on her back and held her tightly. "I don't think it is," I said. "We'd have heard the planes on a still evening like this."

"The last raid was terrible," she said breathlessly. "I was going back to the camp and I couldn't get to a shelter. The plane was right overhead. I thought the rockets were coming straight at me, but they hit the Christian temple."

I stroked her back gently with my right hand. Outside everything was quiet again. "I don't think it's a raid," I said. "Maybe it was some kind of accident. In a moment I'll go and have a look."

"No. Don't leave me - please," she pleaded, beginning to cry.

"All right," I said, hugging her. "I won't leave you. Don't worry. I'll look after you." Gently I removed her glasses and slipped them back into the pocket of her robe. Then I found a handkerchief and pressed it into her hand.

"Dry your eyes, and come and sit on my knee for a minute or two," I said. "Then you can tell me more about yourself."

I sat down and drew her on to my lap, very quickly regretting the invitation, for she was a solid girl and must have weighed nearly as much as I did. However, I put my hand on her thigh to steady her and found it pleasantly soft beneath the smooth silk of the robe.

"How old are you?" I asked.

She dabbed at her eyes with the handkerchief and smiled wanly. "Sorry about that. I didn't mean to make a fool of myself. I suppose I'm more jittery than I realized. It's the uncertainty all the time - it wears you down."

"Yes, and I expect you haven't had any sleep for quite a long time. I really oughtn't to keep you up any longer."

"Oh, no. Please don't go yet," she said, urgently. "I don't feel at all sleepy now. I'd only lie here waiting for another bang,"

"Well, how old are you?" I asked again.

"I'm twenty-three," she replied. "I suppose I must look older."

"On the contrary, I thought you looked younger - though I knew you couldn't be if you were a trained nurse. Where do you live when you're at home?"

"Not far from Matsue at a place called Miho-no-seki."

"Oh, yes. I've been there," I said. "It's the place with the five pine trees, in the old song, isn't it? A lovely view across the harbour."

"Yes, It's very pleasant. But, of course, I'd been away from home when I was doing my training. I was at the Kamo Hospital in Kyoto."

"Did you enjoy your training?" I asked.

"Most of the time," she replied. "And they were very understanding when I had my... trouble."

"That's good," I said, uncertain whether I should encourage her to talk about the breakdown, or whether it would be better to keep her mind off it.

As though reading my thoughts, she said, "I'm all right now, you know - really. But I just get so lonely, when I have time to think." She put her right arm around my shoulders and shifted her bottom slightly on my numbly unappreciative thighs. "You must get lonely sometimes, in your job."

"Yes, I do," I confessed. "Hotel bedrooms, airport departure lounges, station waiting-rooms - they're not the most cheerful places to spend a lot of time in. But I meet a lot of people, too - not that that's any protection against loneliness. I often find I can be more lonely in a crowd than on top of a mountain."

"Yes, I know what you mean," she said, starting to stroke my sleeve with her left hand. "There was a time when I used to like being in a crowd, and going to parties and having lots of friends around me, but now I think I prefer much smaller groups - just one, if he's congenial company." Her face was very close to mine, and the candlelight was reflected softly from her dark brown eyes.

"Do you find me congenial?" I asked.

"Oh, you're very congenial," she purred, and her soft white fingers tentatively touched my cheek. My hand almost involuntarily tightened its grip on her thigh.

I realized then that I had to make a decision. I could leave her now to her lonely bed, or I could stay and give her the physical comfort that she seemed to need even more than my conversation. Or could I? She lacked several of the attributes that normally stirred my sexual interest - a slim waist and a shapely bottom, to name but two — and I didn't want to encourage expectations that couldn't be met to her total satisfaction. However, the novelty of being wooed instead of having to do the wooing ought to compensate for my initial lack of interest, I reflected; and from the chest upward she was really a very attractive girl.

So I decided to stay. And I smiled at the absurdity of my own slightly pompous feeling of virtue at being prepared to do a good turn to a compatriot in distress.

"Why do you smile?" she asked, a little warily.

"Because an hour ago I was feeling very sorry for myself, and wishing I hadn't come on this trip," I lied.

Her fingers strayed into my hair. "Are you married?" she asked.

"I used to be," I said, "but not any more."

"I thought you didn't look married," she said, and now her soft fingertips were stroking my neck. "Do you get very lonely?"

"Sometimes," I replied, deciding to remain passive for a while longer and enjoy the novel sensation of being sought after. "But I've learnt to live with it."

"I don't think I ever want to learn that," she said, and pressed her cheek hard against my neck.

I stroked the back of her silky head very gently. "I shouldn't think you'll have to," I said. "There are a great many people who'd be more than happy to have your company. Your only problem will be to make a choice."

"Do you really think so?" she asked, tossing back her head to look up at me.

I kissed the tip of her nose. "Of course I do. And you know it, too - though being down and discouraged may have made you doubt it for a moment. We all feel like that, sometimes."

She kissed my cheek three times, with warm, moist lips, and then looked up at me questioningly. I smiled and put my hand behind her head, drawing it towards me until our lips met. Her mouth was eager, and almost immediately her tongue was thrusting between my teeth. I felt her fingers unbuttoning my shirt front, and soon they were stroking my chest.

In the breathing space that punctuated the kisses I saw that her eyes were shining with intense excitement. Then her lips sought mine a second time, more fiercely than the first. I thrust my right hand beneath the fold of her crimson robe and found the naked flesh of her breast, soft and smooth and exquisitely resilient to my touch. The nipple stiffened at the first caress of my fingertips, and another stiffening reassured me that I needn't be afraid of disappointing her.

Disengaging her lips she slid off my lap and stood in front of me, looking down with shining eyes. Then, with a slightly dramatic movement, she flung open the robe and let it fall around her feet. In the warm glow of the firelight her naked flesh had an almost Occidental pinkness. Her breasts were delightfully proportioned but the plumpness below them was a little disappointing. Touch, I decided, was the sense from which I could hope to gain the greatest pleasure. I stood up quickly, and almost fell against her, because my legs had gone numb with the weight that had been pressing down upon them. Clutching her by the shoulders I held on for a moment, and pressed my lips to the side of her neck so that she shouldn't see the grimace of agony on my face. Then I sank slowly to my knees, planting a few kisses on her breasts and her firm, surprisingly flat belly on the way. I pressed my face against her warm flesh, weighing her heavy buttocks in the palms of my hands, and murmured, "Scotland has no scenery to equal this."

She stooped and kissed the top of my head, running her fingers through my hair. "Flatterer," she said. "I'm glad you didn't see me six weeks ago, before they started, cutting down the rations. At this rate it'll only be another week or two before I'm back to what I was before... before my breakdown. That was when I started putting on weight."

"Lucky you had some reserves," I said. "Anyhow, I'm a voluptuary - I like my sensations in good measure. Turn around."

She obeyed, and I very gently sank my teeth into the soft hemisphere of her bottom. I heard and felt her long, shuddering gasp of delight, and now I was ready for anything. Sensation had returned to my tingling legs and I was able to stand upright again. I blew out the candles. "What about precautions?" I asked.

"I'm on the tablet," she replied. "Mainly because it makes things more bearable when I have my period."

In the flickering glow of the log-fire she stripped off my clothes with experienced fingers. "Mm....I like being undressed by you," I said, as her soft fingers slid under the waistband of my briefs and pushed them down over my hips.

"You men are just like babies. You love having things done for you. I noticed that when I was on the men's wards," she said.

"We love it when someone like you is doing them," I said, stepping out of the pants. "You'd have noticed a different reaction if you'd been flat-chested and cross-eyed, with cold fingers."

I put my arm around her waist and led her over to the bed. She lay down immediately, catching my hands to pull me on top of her, and her eagerness was unmistakable. My own slight hesitation may have been an advantage, for I was able to keep her in apparent ecstasy for more than half-an-hour before I shot my bolt. And then she very quickly teased me into action again with the subtle stimulation of her lips.

The fire had faded out by the time we had exhausted ourselves, and we were glad to push back the bedclothes and snuggle underneath them. Hiroko very quickly fell asleep, but I lay for a little while, listening to the contented rhythm of her breathing and satisfied to feel the total relaxation of her body, softly straddling my own.

Then, suddenly, I felt a strong, compelling desire to be with Miranda. So urgent was the feeling that after a time I was tempted to wake Hiroko and begin making love to her again, in the hope that that would assuage it. As I lay there in the darkness everything around me seemed totally unreal: the only reality was my memory of Miranda.

I suppose that if I'd grown up in a Western society I might have felt guilt because I'd just had physical intercourse with another woman, but that was the feeling farthest from my mind. If anything, I was feeling a little bit virtuous for having had enough physical tenderness to spare for someone who needed it. There wouldn't be any the less for Miranda.

What was really disturbing me was the realization that the physical pleasure I'd just experienced was something I could have taken or could equally well have refused, but the need to be with Miranda was a compulsion that couldn't any longer be denied. I was back with total commitment to one person, and this time it was I who had created the gap that separated her from me.

CHAPTER 11

The explosion that had frightened Hiroko into my arms had killed General Johnston. He was leaving the Chancellery after an interview with Knox when his car blew up. The official communiqué said the bomb had been planted by English agents. And the funeral was conducted with great pomp and military parade amid the dismal squalling of the bagpipes - although I noticed that the religious ceremony, performed according to the Buddhist rite, began only after the crowds and the dignitaries had departed.

Knox assumed supreme command of all the Scottish forces, with the title of Generalissimo, and Mackie became his Chief of Staff.

Two days after the funeral the media were summoned to a special briefing, at which, we were told, a new and important development in the military situation would be announced. For reasons which were not made plain in the invitation, we would be taken to the briefing by car. So we duly assembled at the Chancellery to join a little convoy commanded by McSkimming, now promoted to Captain.

I found myself sitting beside a recent addition to the Press Corps, a stocky man with bristling eyebrows and close-cropped hair, who told me that his name was Shinroku Iguchi. By his accent it was quite evident that he came from the Federated States, and I asked him for which paper he worked.

"Independent News Services," he replied. I had never heard of them. "We're a pretty new outfit," he went on. "That's why we want to be in on the big news that's hard to get. It took a lot of trouble and a lot of money to get in here, I can tell you. But you must have jumped through the same hoops."

"I had some good contacts," I said.

"Do you know what they're taking us to see today?" he asked.

"I've no idea," I replied.

"It must be something to do with the Mongolians that have been coming in," he said. "I saw one of their aircraft on the runway the night I arrived."

"Are you sure it was one of theirs?" I asked. "I haven't seen any of them around - and they're not exactly easy to miss."

He laughed harshly. "It was one of theirs, all right - a Giant Panda Transport. And I shouldn't think it was carrying tins of baby food. But maybe that's what we're going to find out today."

"I can't think why they should have decided to come in at this late stage in the game," I said. "They don't usually back losers; and it'll take more than a few plane-loads of weapons, however sophisticated, to tip the balance now. There might have been an outside chance before Johnston was killed -but I suppose they couldn't have known that was going to happen when they made their decision to intervene."

"Maybe Knox wouldn't have accepted their help any sooner," said my companion. "I've heard that he's a fanatical Christian, which ought to make him anti-Collectivist. But I suppose he's getting desperate, now that nobody else will help him. We've seen that happen all too often in the past. A small state gets up to its ears in the swamp and looks around for a helping hand, and then – click! - before it knows what's happened the manacles are round its wrists."

"I suppose some of them prefer that to drowning in the swamp," I remarked.

He looked at me suspiciously. "There are some things worse than death," he said, "but I suppose you can't expect these pinkies to understand that. They have no democratic tradition."

"Well, they didn't have much opportunity to develop one when they were colonies," I said.

"That's very true. You East Asians have a lot to answer for. You were far too slow in introducing democratic institutions in your empires. The world might be a whole lot safer for democracy if you'd got a move on, before the Collectivists had a chance to start winning the hearts and minds of the discontented peasantry. We learnt that lesson in South Greece, trying to clear up the mess that the Honanese left behind them." His round face glowed with moral earnestness.

"A lot of people would say that you were trying to do the same kind of thing there yourselves - having your own empire, and not bothering too much about democracy," I remarked.

"And a lot of people would be wrong," he replied belligerently. "I've heard that kind of Collectivist claptrap, and it makes me sick. Of course we had our problems with the Greeks and some of the ones on our side were crooked, like so many of these pinkies. And of course they couldn't have proper elections. How in thunder could they, when there was fighting going on over two-thirds of the country? But one thing's sure, they had more freedom in those days than they'll ever have under the Salonica Government.

“And that's what it was all about. Our boys were in there to defend freedom, because freedom is indivisible. Those college youngsters who were so quick to call their own country 'imperialist' maybe couldn't understand that, because they'd never known what it was like to lose their freedom."

"I thought quite a few of them lost it - in jail, after the demonstrations," I said.

"My son lost his life when the Blacks broke through at Thermopylae," Iguchi replied. "He was a fine young man - only twenty years old - and he believed in what he was fighting for. I know that because he used to write in his letters how proud he was to be defending those poor people against the dreadful things that the Blacks were doing to them.”

Tears were glistening in his eyes. "I'm very sorry," I murmured. "It must have been a terrible blow to you."

"It broke his mother's heart," he said. "She couldn't see the other side to it - that Dorgon would have been proud to die for freedom. She just couldn't understand, and it's made her very bitter. I suppose you can’t expect a woman to see the broader picture. But I try to carry on the good work in my own way." Then, quite abruptly, he changed the subject, asking, "Have you seen much of this war?"

"I was here at the beginning," I replied, "and I've seen most of it, except during the lull in the summer."

"What do you think of the Scottish army? Have they still got a chance?"

"They've been brave fighters, and under Johnston they were clever, too; but now that he's gone I'm not sure what will happen. And their firepower is getting weaker all the time, while the Government forces are getting stronger. Apart from that, they must be pretty short of ammunition, not to mention food. I don't know what little present the Mongolians may have brought them, but it can’t make very much difference."

We continued to talk about the military situation as the car jolted, and lurched over an increasingly rugged road. Eventually the convoy came to a halt and we found ourselves on a wooded hillside, looking south over a wide valley. Down below I saw signs of military activity, and guessed that we must be fairly near the front line.

Among the trees was a sandbagged and heavily camouflaged emplacement, containing what looked like a small rocket-launcher, about two metres in length. Behind it, in the open, a truck was parked, carrying what I recognized as a radio detection rangefinder, and this was connected to the launcher by a cable. Several Mongolians in civilian overalls stood around.

"It's their new Black Dragon ground-to-air missile," said Iguchi. He put his hand in the pocket of his fur-lined overcoat and brought out a small but complicated-looking camera. One of the Mongolians noticed it immediately and began to gesticulate in an agitated fashion.

McSkimining ran across to us, saying apologetically, "Our Mongolian friends don't want any photographs, please. Their equipment is still on the secret list."

Then he asked us to gather round, and we stood, stamping our feet on the frozen ground, while a Scottish Colonel told us that the Mongolian Government had made available defensive anti-aircraft equipment of the kind which we would shortly see demonstrated, so that the Scottish people could once again maintain the integrity of their skies against the invader. 'Advisers' had come with the equipment to instruct the Scottish artillerymen who would be operating it.

"A likely story," muttered Iguchi. "Pinkies wouldn't understand that box of tricks in a hundred years."

A Honanese reporter asked how many rocket launchers had been made available, and the colonel replied that there were enough to destroy any English aircraft that came within range of the Scottish lines.

"What is their range?" I asked.

"That's a military secret," he replied. "But you're soon going to see how effective they are. Every day at just about this time the English send a helicopter, to take a look at what we're up to." He glanced towards the two Mongolians operating the rangefinder and one of them signalled with his hand. "Yes, it's on its way now."

We all turned our eyes towards the southern horizon, but it was a couple of minutes before we could see the black speck against the blue.

"It could have been taken out already," said the colonel, "but we'll let it come a little closer so that you can get a ringside view. And if anyone wants to take a picture of the death-blow, he's very welcome - but no close-ups of the equipment, please."

Several pairs of binoculars were being passed around, and at that moment a pair was handed to me. I raised the glasses to my eyes, but it was several seconds before I could find the right sector of sky on which to train them. Then, suddenly, the helicopter appeared in the lenses, quite large now, and unmistakably a Hellcat. My thoughts flew back to that morning in Selkirk and the screams of the scattering crowd of fugitives, and I watched the growing shape of the gunship with fierce anticipation.

Close at hand I heard the report of the launcher but kept my eyes fastened on its target. The Hellcat had just begun to bank, swinging around to the east, when the rocket struck its tail-boom and exploded in a dazzling orange flash. The bull-nosed cabin hurtled to earth like a meteor, trailing flame and smoke, and my feelings of jubilant revenge were rapidly replaced by the sickening thought of a young man's body wrapped in a blanket of fire. A triumphant cheer went up from the watching Scottish soldiers. It wasn't my quarrel, but I knew that if it had been I would have cheered along with them. Compassion, I feared, was a luxury derived from my neutrality.

The colonel was beaming with satisfaction and explaining to anyone who cared to listen how aerial superiority had now been taken away from the English. "I can't understand why they should have demonstrated it to us, instead of springing it as a surprise in a major engagement," Iguchi remarked to me. I noticed that he had used the cover of the excitement to take a surreptitious snap of the rocket-launcher.

"Maybe they know they haven't the strength to exploit whatever advantage this might give them, and they're hoping the demonstration will frighten off an impending attack and win them a bit of time," I suggested.

The radio operator from the scout car that had accompanied our convoy came running up to McSkimming and handed him a message. The young man read it quickly and called out to us, "I've had a message from the Chancellor. He wants you all to return to Perth immediately, to hear about a most important development that has just taken place."

As we walked back to the cars I joked to Iguchi, "These fellows have no news sense. If they had they'd know better than to release two big stories on the same day."

For a moment he looked blank, but then he laughed and said, "Oh, yes. You've got a point there. I hope they leave us enough time to file our reports."

On the return journey McSkimming travelled in the car with Iguchi and me, sitting beside the driver. He talked over his shoulder in an excited but rather vague way about the victorious new strategy that could be expected, now that Knox had taken over the command. Iguchi questioned him, but I soon stopped listening to their rambling conversation and looked out of the window at the bleak, sunlit landscape.

My thoughts went back to that warm, autumn evening when Miranda and I had looked over the sunlit fields outside Selkirk, and I wondered how long it would be before I saw her again. It was a long time since I had thought of any one place as "home", but now I realized that wherever she was would be home for me. And I resolved to give that feeling some grounding in reality at the earliest possible moment - if Miranda would agree. I even contemplated the possibility of taking a job in the office and settling down in Nagoya, if Miranda would consent to come with me. There was a fishing village near Yokosuka that might not be too far out of the city, if I was lucky enough to find an empty house there.

Suddenly I became aware that the car was slowing down. We seemed to be entering a village.

"Where are we?" I asked McSkimming.

"It's a little place called Auchterarder," he replied. "Something seems to be holding us up. I expect it's a flock of sheep." He wound down his window and stuck out his head, in an attempt to see past the scout car in front of us. A breeze blew through the open window, bringing with it a strange, unpleasant smell that I couldn't put a name to. There was wood smoke in the odour, but mingled with something else that I thought might be an unfamiliar chemical.

We rounded a bend and saw immediately the reason for the delay. The road traversed an open space - the village green, I suppose - and a crowd that thronged it was spilling over on to the roadway. They were paying little heed to the convoy, so rapt was their attention to the spectacle in their midst. At first I thought it was simply a bonfire, but then the breeze shifted, blowing the greyish-brown smoke to one side and I saw a human body, sheathed in flame. The head, covered with long white hair, was hanging down, but suddenly it jerked erect in a spasm of agony and I saw the face. It was the face of an old woman, round and wrinkled and horribly reddened in the heat. She opened her mouth and uttered a scream that pierced through the surrounding noise like a laser beam of pure pain.

McSkimming turned and bade the driver blow his horn to hasten the convoy on its way. "Aren't we going to stop and see this?" Iguchi demanded. "It looks like a story to me."

"We've no time to waste," said McSkimming as the car began to pick up speed. His face was flushed and he was clearly upset.

"What's going on there?" I asked. "What are they doing."

"Burning a witch," McSkimming replied, not turning his head to look at us. "It's not very pleasant, I know, but in times like these it's to be expected."

"But isn't that against the law? It must be nearly a hundred and fifty years since the colonial government put a stop to it," I said.

McSkimming stared straight ahead as he answered, "The custom was abolished by the imperial power, though it's sometimes been carried on in secret. Chancellor Knox has allowed it to be restored because it's part of our national tradition - and there's been an outbreak of witchcraft that's been dangerous to public morale. He says that true democracy means allowing the people to decide, and burning's the penalty the people want to see enforced. You can be sure the woman was properly tried and found guilty by an ecclesiastical court."

"But don't you think it's barbaric? And doing it in public - it's obscene," said Iguchi.

I saw McSkimming's neck reddening. "It's a horrible punishment, but then so is the crime," he replied. "And our religion says that it's necessary. Besides," he continued, turning to look at us, his boyish face contorted with emotion, "it's no worse than the effect of liquid fire bombs, which your countries manufacture and use in war."

We said no more. But when we were clear of the village and speeding through the countryside again Iguchi muttered, to me, "I'm beginning to see why you Japanese felt you had to hang on so long. They're not much better than savages - just out of the caves. It's the same in Greece, you know. My boy told me in one of his letters about recapturing a village where the Blacks had been, and finding these people tied to trees - men and women. They'd been slashed open with knives and left to bleed to death. They're savages, whatever the pinky-lovers may say about their ancient culture and the moral quality of their religion. No wonder our missionaries couldn't make much headway with them."

"It was a savage thing to do, " I said, the face of the old woman still before my eyes, "but that doesn't mean they 're savages. I saw the body of a young man who'd been killed in my own home town - when I was covering the Southern Hokkaido troubles, a couple of years ago. He'd been shot eleven times in the arms and legs and left to die, by people that I grew up with. If they're savages then I'm a savage, too."

All the way back to Perth I couldn't get the woman's face out of my mind. But the episode was quickly forgotten when we heard what Knox had to tell us. He was looking very pleased with himself when we were ushered into his office at the Chancellery, and he beamed benevolently as he gestured to us to be seated.

"Gentlemen, I received this morning an historic communication, which marks a turning-point in Scotland's struggle for freedom," he announced, holding up a sheet of paper in his right hand. "Through the good offices of a representative of the International Yellow Lotus, I have received an offer from the English Prime Minister, to begin negotiations about a settlement."

A murmur of astonishment ran along the row of reporters, and even McSkimming looked surprised.

Knox continued, "The message says that if we were to ask for talks our request would be considered sympathetically. You will observe that Mr. Serjeant, who declared so boldly that he would never negotiate, doesn't want to be seen to make the first move."

"Does the message say anything about terms, Chancellor?" asked Iguchi.

There was a long pause, while Knox looked intently at the piece of paper and then threw it down on his desk with a dramatic flourish. "It does indeed," he said. "Even though his message is a sign that he sees defeat staring him in the face, Mr. Serjeant cannot bring himself to recognize the reality of the situation. Scotland is a free and independent nation, born in blood - though that was not of her own choosing; but he says he wants to talk about a return to the situation before the Declaration of Edinburgh, as if nothing had happened."

"And what will your reply be, Chancellor?" asked a Honanese reporter.

"My reply," said Knox, putting the tips of his podgy fingers together, "will be very simple - and I will leave it to you gentlemen to deliver it for me, since Mr. Serjeant hasn't seen fit to correspond with me directly. My reply is this: When the English Prime Minister asks me, as the Chancellor of Scotland, to negotiate with him about the ending of this tragic war between our two peoples and the safe withdrawal of English soldiers beyond their own frontier, I will be happy to do so. Until that time, I have nothing to say to him."

"Would you not even be interested in talking about a truce, Chancellor?" asked Iguchi.

Knox stared at him as though he had uttered an obscenity. "I have just told you the only basis on which I am prepared to negotiate," he said. "I don't change my mind in the next breath - or even in the next week, like Mr. Serjeant."

"There is one other thing I ought to say to you, "he went on. "When your reports are published Mr. Serjeant will doubtless deny that he ever sent a message to me. He took great pains to ensure that there was nothing in writing; but I have here, on this paper, a transcript of the tape-recording of my conversation with the Yellow Lotus representative, Mr. K'ang, which I will be happy to show you."

Serjeant did, indeed, deny that he had ever sent a message to Knox, but nobody believed him. Whether he did send one, or whether the whole story was one of Knox's inventions is still uncertain, for the truth was known only to the two of them and Mr. K'ang, who said nothing, for fear of imperilling the neutral status of his organisation. But the effect of Knox's revelation was devastating, even if not in quite the way that he had intended. Two days later Serjeant's government was overthrown by the military under General O'Neill, who took over the running of the country, and the war.

CHAPTER 12

The forward observation post was dug deeply into a hillside, and we had to walk in a crouching posture along the dark, narrow tunnel that led into it. Being slightly claustrophobic by nature, I didn't enjoy the experience. It must have been even less enjoyable for Generalissimo Knox, who came near to getting stuck at one of the bends.

I learnt from McSkimming that Knox had included me in his party because he looked on me as a kind of mascot. I had been present at his greatest successes and I had, in his mind, saved him from serious injury in the refugee camp. Now I was to witness yet another triumph, his first great victory as a military commander - the masterstroke that was going to relieve the pressure on the Scottish forces.

We were packed tightly into the observation post. As well as Knox, McSkimming and myself there were two other staff officers and a radio operator with a walkie-talkie, who also had a field telephone in his corner. The gloom was relieved a little by an evil-smelling oil lamp; but the main source of both light and interest was the slit about a metre and a half in length and twenty centimetres high, through which we were to survey the scene of the impending action - or our particular corner of it. Knox had spread out a map on the sill, and he was in genial humour as he showed me our position on it.

"Do you see this valley, young man?" he asked, tracing the contours with his fat forefinger. "That's what you can see, straight in front of your nose. It's called the Crook of Devon. The other arm of the crook goes off to the right, behind our own forward line, which is on the far side of the hilltops. That valley is like a pistol pointed at the weak spot in the enemy's front."

He slapped my shoulder with a heavy hand. "In five minutes from now our brave boys will storm down there, carrying all before them. When they get to the bottom they'll swing round to the west, mopping up any resistance they meet, till they take the bridge across the Forth at Stirling." His finger jabbed at the map. "Then we'll see how long their Second Division will stand at Greenloaning, when they know their retreat's been cut off to the south."

From the map I could see the possibilities inherent in the plan; but I wondered whether the half-starved, ill-equipped troops I had seen on our drive to the front were strong enough or numerous enough to carry it out. "What about their Armoured Brigade? Mightn't it mount a counter-attack from Dunblane?" I asked,

"A very good question, young man," Knox replied, patting my shoulder. "We'll have to enlist you in the General Staff." The two staff officers echoed his laugh sycophantically. "There are two answers to that one," he continued. "First, we're going to be attacking simultaneously along the whole length of our line, from Newburgh to Comrie." His finger traced an arc across the map.

"By the time they realize that the main thrust is here they'll have committed their reserves, including the armour, elsewhere - probably at Blackford, where we'll be expecting them."

He lowered his face towards mine, his eyes twinkling behind his spectacles with delight at his own cunning. "The second reason is even more important," he said. "Do you know what day this is?"

I was able to answer that because McSkimming had already told me, "It's your Christmas Day, " I replied.

Knox beamed. "It is, indeed," he said. "And a merry Christmas to us all. This is the one day of the year above all others on which the English won't expect us to attack them. They'll be indulging themselves on an extra liquor ration and looking forward to their Christmas dinner. At this very moment the pigs and the oxen will be turning on the spits. My sources tell me that they brought up whole train-loads of animals the day before yesterday. And now the men will be crowding around the cooking-fires, keeping themselves warm and thinking of nothing but the moment when they're going to fill their mess-tins."

The officers chuckled appreciatively. "But they'll never carve the meat off those carcasses," he continued, pointing through the slit towards the sky-line, “because any minute now they're going to have some uninvited guests. Tonight our own brave boys will be enjoying the feast they've so thoughtfully provided. I'm afraid it'll have gone cold by then, but there's work to be done in the meantime."

I decided to push my luck and ask a dangerous question. “Was the strategy for this attack worked out before General Johnston's tragic death?" I enquired.

Knox pursed his lips and paused for a moment before answering. "There is something which I think you ought to know, young man," he said, "though I trust that for the moment you will treat it in confidence. But one day the full record of these historic events must surely be made known."

He lowered his face towards mine once again, and his little eyes were narrowed and intense. "General Johnston was a traitor to Scotland," he declared. "I had long been puzzled, as you must have been, by the defeats and. losses suffered by our brave soldiers after their first victories, when they demonstrated their superiority over the enemy. But it wasn't until Johnston began openly spreading defeatism, and urging a policy that would have led us straight to surrender, that I awoke to what had been happening. I blame myself now for not having seen it sooner."

I noticed that McSkimming and the other officers weren't really listening to this momentous revelation, and guessed that they must have heard the story already.

Knox went on, "There was only one fault in our army, and that was the treachery of its commander. The English must have been aware of every move before we made it. Maybe one day we'll find out what reward they promised him for his services. But he got his reward all right - he got his reward."

"Then it wasn't the English that killed him?" I asked, knowingly.

"In war there are many distasteful necessities," he replied with a sigh. "You can understand that it wouldn't have been good for morale if there had been a sudden revelation of what had been going on. Many of the men thought quite highly of Johnston, and it wouldn't have done to shatter their faith without warning. When the tide has turned again, of course, the truth will have to be made known. And all the evidence will then be available, so that the people can judge for themselves the decisions that were taken on their behalf. I will submit myself humbly to their judgment, in this as in everything."

I wondered whether he had persuaded himself to believe the story he was telling me, or whether he was still aware of the envy or the fear that had driven him to murder Johnston. And as his cold, blue eyes gazed at me from behind his spectacles I felt a tremor of fear myself. He was capable of doing the same to anyone else whom his diseased mind saw as a threat to his security.

From somewhere outside on the bleak hills a strange, wailing sound assaulted our ears. I had heard it often enough by this time to recognize the bagpipes. But now I began to understand, as I had never been able to before, why so strident an instrument could summon up so much enthusiasm among its hearers. Out there, in the face of danger and death, it was the voice of the tribe, the authentic call of their ancestors, binding them together with the comforting certainty that they were part of something that could never die. For a moment I felt myself wanting to be one of them, sharing in the glory of their madness.

I raised the binoculars that McSkimming had lent me, and saw little groups of men apparently rising out of the earth all along the hillsides to the south. There were hundreds of them, and as they began to move down into the valley I noticed that each group seemed to consist of three men, one armed with a rifle and bayonet and the others with broadswords or axes. They all wore kilts, and I wished that I could have identified the various tartans.

McSkimming nudged me. "Do you see that group of fir-trees?" he asked, pointing straight ahead. "There's an English outpost in the sheep-fold to the left of them."

I trained my glasses on what looked like a pile of stones, and as I did so a pin-point of flame flickered on its centre. The valley echoed with the rattle of machine-gunfire. I saw a Highlander stumble, fall and lie still. One of his comrades immediately bent down and picked up his rifle, running on towards the sheep-fold until he, too, was hit and the rifle passed to the third man in the group.

A second machine-gun somewhere to the east, out of my line of vision, joined in the firing and more of the running figures fell to the ground. Now the Highlanders began to take cover and return the fire. I noticed a group of five taking up position behind a hillock some four hundred metres from the sheepfold. They were carrying what looked like a length of pipe, and I guessed that it must be a mortar. While they were setting up their weapon two Scottish light machine-guns began firing, but without any apparent effect. Then the mortar fired, but its bomb exploded well beyond the enemy position. Knox shouted angrily in English, banging the sill with his fist in exasperation.

As the mortar was being reloaded I swung my glasses round towards the sheep-fold again. A movement on the ground some ten metres away from it caught my eye, and I saw that it was one of the Highlanders crawling steadily forward on his belly. Another mortar bomb exploded, a few metres short of its target this time. Then the Highlander stood up. He was no more than a centimetre high in my lens, but I could see the throwing action of his arm as he hurled a grenade. There was a red flash, a puff of smoke, and the machine-gun stopped firing.

"What happened?" asked Knox, who had been watching the mortar.

"One of your men got close to them and threw a grenade," I replied. He beamed jubilantly and slapped my shoulder.

“They're unstoppable, these brave boys," he said. "Major McSkimming, find out who that man was. We'll give him the Cross of St. Andrew when this day's work is over."

There was a distant bang, followed by a high-pitched scream that made me duck my head instinctively. On more than one occasion in this war I had been too close for comfort to the seventy-six millimetre shells of the field guns. The projectile exploded about a half a kilometre away, in the valley below us, and it was followed by three more in rapid succession. A solitary Scottish gun somewhere to the rear of us replied to the salvo.

Now that the machine-gun post had been overrun, the infantrymen were rapidly moving out of sight down the valley, and the shell fire followed them in a series of diminishing eruptions. We could no longer make out any details through the haze of smoke that drifted between the hills, but the steady rattle and thump of continuous firing told us that the battle was spreading.

The field telephone buzzed, and we watched impatiently while the signalman wrote down the message. He handed it to Knox, whose face broke into a triumphant beam as he read it. "Great news from General Mackie," he said. "Our brave boys have broken through the enemy at Glenfarg."

McSkimming's eyebrows shot up in surprise. "We really must have caught them with their backs turned," he exclaimed. "They had armour down there - two Daimyos and at least four Tartars."

Knox shook his head disapprovingly. "No armour in the world can prevail against the sword of the spirit, young man. Those who fight for Scotland must fight in faith. It's faith that has set those brave Macdonalds and Macgregors on the road to Kinross. Now we can roll up their whole right flank. O'Neil would have done better to stay with his army than start playing at being prime minister in London.

"As for us, we must be getting back to headquarters, for there'll be nothing more to be seen here. And we can't expect young Mackie to do our work for us, and handle the whole army on his own in his first battle - though he's not doing so badly. He's not doing badly at all."

Knox was in high good humour as he moved his great bulk towards the entrance. At that moment we heard the roar of a jet and the bunker shook to the thud of an explosion. Looking through the observation slit I saw a Typhoon disappearing down the valley through the drifting smoke.

"He came from the north," said McSkimming, with a look of bewilderment.

Knox's face was red with anger as he stood blocking the doorway. "Where were the Mongolians?" he shouted. "Why didn't they shoot it down? That's what they're supposed to be here for, the treacherous atheists."

As he spoke he was propelled forward into the arms of McSkimming, his expression changing rapidly from anger to alarm, "Oh, I beg your pardon, sir," exclaimed the cause of his discomfiture, a steel-helmeted captain, who had come down the tunnel at speed with his head lowered, and had struck his generalissimo squarely in the small of the back. I recognized him as the Honanese mercenary in command of the escort that had accompanied us to the front.

"The plane, sir," he said, straightening up. "It's knocked out the Mongolian rangefinder, but it missed the rocket launcher. It came from the rear - must have flown in from the sea and across the hills to baffle the rangefinder. I thought perhaps you'd be wanting to get back to headquarters now, sir. We hadn't reckoned on enemy air activity."

Knox leaned on McSkimming's shoulder to steady himself and straightened his spectacles. "I trust our Mongolian friends in other parts of the front will be more successful with their rockets. It's a bad soldier that let's himself be surprised from the rear. Eyes and ears would be more reliable than their electrical devices, it seems to me."

The field telephone buzzed again. The signalman said something in English which included General Mackie's name, and Knox took the receiver from him. The red flush drained from his cheeks as he listened and his hand began to tremble. He said what sounded like a question, and the three Scottish officers immediately looked alarmed. Then he listened, the muscles of his face twitching with emotion. When he spoke again his voice was hoarse and dejected.

Knox handed back the telephone to the signalman and for a moment remained silent, fumbling in the pocket of his tunic for a handkerchief. Then he removed his spectacles, wiped his eyes and mopped his forehead. He spoke a few words in English and the three Scottish officers uttered exclamations of alarm. The Honanese and I exchanged puzzled glances.

Knox replaced his spectacles and turned towards me. He seemed to be beginning to recover his composure, and he spoke very slowly. "Young man," he said, "it is with great sorrow I have to tell you that once again Scotland has been betrayed. English forces have landed at Perth and are advancing on our rear. They have chosen the holiest day of the year to launch this onslaught on their fellow-Christians, and history will record its judgment on their action. We have a hard fight ahead of us, but with the help of Christ and his Holy Mother Scotland will win through."

He gestured to the Honanese to lead the way. "Now we must go and join our brave General Mackie, to take over the direction of the army and re-group it for what must, I fear, be another retreat. He'll meet us at Auchterarder."

As we moved into the tunnel Knox said, "It wouldn't be fair to blame young Mackie for this tragic reverse. He has had very little experience of battle. I must accept a part of the responsibility myself for having placed too heavy a burden on his shoulders. Even though I had some doubts about the strategy, I let him take complete command of this operation. I myself have been only a spectator. No, he's not entirely to blame."

Out on the hillside in the cold, invigorating air we could see the wreckage of the rangefinder a few hundred metres away on the opposite slope. The survivors of the crew were busying themselves around the rocket launcher. Our little convoy of four scout cars, the first and last containing the men of the escort, came bouncing up the rough track to collect us.

I raised my binoculars to have a last look down the valley, where the smoke was beginning to clear. The dark specks on the ground were too far away to make out which were still alive and which would never move again. I was about to turn round and get into the car when a movement caught my attention. Quickly I adjusted the focus of the powerful glasses and saw that it was a tracked machine-gun carrier advancing up the valley.

"Major McSkimming," I called out, "there's something happening down there."

He ran to my side, raising his own field-glasses to his eyes, and together we stared southward. Now I could make out a swarm of dark, ant-like specks following the armoured vehicle.

"What's happening? What's the matter?" shouted Knox, who had seated himself beside the driver of his car, parked a little way below the crest of the hill. "Don't tell me our boys are pulling back - not the MacDougalls and the Gordons." He began to climb out again.

"They're not retreating, sir," said McSkimming, lowering his glasses. "There must be none of them left. It's the English coming up the valley."

Knox turned pale and traced the sign of a cross in front of himself with his right hand. "Martyred for Scotland," he said. "They have their glory for ever more."

I shared the back seat of the generalissimo's scout car with McSkimming and the radio operator. We rattled and bounded over the deeply rutted road, heading towards the north-west. About five minutes after we set out there was a loud explosion from the direction in which we had come, and I looked back to see a pillar of black smoke curling up into the sky.

"That must have been the Mongolians getting rid of the rest of their rockets," said McSkimming.

A few minutes later we heard the sound of a plane in the clouds to the north but it soon faded into the background rumble of distant artillery fire that accompanied us whichever way we turned. All the same, I kept an anxious eye on the skyline. In this bleak, open countryside we would be a perfect target for any passing fighter or helicopter, and I had no desire to share in Knox's 'martyrdom.'

Memories of Miranda came flooding into my mind: the first moment I saw her; the night ride to Newcastle; waking up beside her on that sunny morning in Selkirk; crouching among the ruins while the helicopter passed above our heads. What, I asked myself, was I doing, driving through these empty hills, scoured of even the sheep that would have inhabited them in normal times, alongside a lunatic who was the prime target for every piece of ordnance within thirty miles? The only right and reasonable place for me was in her company.

Incongruously, I remembered the little devotional song that the dancing monk, Kuya, used to sing a thousand years ago:

A far off, distant land

Is Paradise,

I've heard men say;

But those who want to go
Can reach it in a day.

I could be in Paradise before nightfall, if I could get to an aeroplane, or any other form of transport that would take me to London. But the chances were that an aeroplane would get to me first, and then...? It wasn't the thought of death that appalled me, so much as the realization that I might never see Miranda again, never hear her soft, melodious voice or thrill to the touch of her warm flesh. She was the centre of my life and everything else was peripheral.

It was incredible how long it had taken me to realize that, and now it was probably too late. One bomb, one rocket, and all those subtle harmonies of mind and body that we had discovered together would be like an old, forgotten tune, never to be played again. My teeth rattled as the scout car went over a boulder, and I swore to myself that if I survived this day I'd ask the editor to give me a job as an art critic. Then, at least, I'd know the lunatics I was dealing with were harmless.

We were turning north, now, into a wider, gentler valley, and here the sounds of battle were much closer and more distinct. I guessed that the fighting couldn't be much more than a kilometre away, and there were clouds of smoke to be seen on the south-western horizon.

"The English must have broken through at Blackford," McSkimming muttered anxiously.

Having come on to a metalled road, the cars picked up speed and raced ahead. Over his shoulder Knox instructed the radio operator to try to contact General Mackie, but there was no reply. "If he's reached Auchterarder when we get there we'll withdraw to Crieff together," said Knox, "but if he hasn't we'll go on alone, and take as many of the men as we can disengage. We could take the road through the hills and get behind the English to Blairgowrie. Call up Colonel Logan at Tullibardine. His Glasgow Rifles can cover the retreat."

There was a shout from the car behind. I looked back and saw one of the staff officers standing up and pointing at the sky. Following the direction of his finger I made out the growing shape of a helicopter swooping down from the clouds,

The cars screeched to a halt and we ran for cover in the ditches by the sides of the road, while the soldiers in the rear car mounted their light machine-gun on a stone wall. The gunship had seen us, and came in low to the attack. Crouching down I watched while the machine-gunner opened fire, one of his comrades holding the weapon's bipod steady on the wall. The Hellcat's cannon dipped and the red streaks of its tracer shells rapped out a dotted line that met the earth in a series of small explosions. A fragment of metal, or it may have been stone, zipped past my head and I dropped on to my stomach and hugged the sodden, decaying vegetation in the bottom of the ditch.

When I cautiously looked up again the helicopter had passed over and was beginning to swing round. Where the machine-gun had been the wall had disintegrated into a pile of rubble. One soldier's head and shoulders protruded from beneath it and another lay in a crumpled, blood-stained heap beside him. The two survivors were propped against the wall looking stunned. I quickly ducked down again and lay still as the gunship came in for another attack. This time its projectiles tore into the first two scout cars, setting them on fire.

It seemed clear to me that the ditch wasn't going to offer much protection if the helicopter crew decided to be thorough about eliminating us, and so I looked around desperately for some alternative. About thirty metres ahead I saw something that gave me hope. A little stream ran under the road, through a culvert. In there, I thought, we might have a chance of survival.

"Look! There's a culvert under the road. Let's try and get to it," I shouted, setting off at a crouching trot along the ditch. Overhead I heard the throbbing of the gunship's engine as it approached once more. Throwing myself down I tried to press my body into the side of the ditch. A salvo of shells ripped into the road only metres away from me, and I was enveloped in a cloud of smoke and grit. McSkimming had been following close behind me, and when I stopped he fell across my legs. A black box I had seen him snatch from under the seat when he leapt out of the scout car fell from his hand and tumbled along the ditch beside me. Its lid sprang open revealing a richly ornamented golden circlet that dazzled my eyes.

"What in the world is that?" I asked, stretching out my hand to pick it up. As I turned to hand it back to him I could see that tears were glistening in his eyes.

"It's the crown," he replied. "If the battle had been won we were going straight to Scone tomorrow morning - that's where the kings of Scotland were crowned in olden times."

"Let's get to the culvert now," I said, "before the helicopter turns again."

We ran the last few metres with anxious eyes on the wheeling gunship, which was making ready for another attacking run. Up to our knees in water, Knox, McSkimming, the driver and I crowded under the roadway, to find the Honanese captain and two of his men already crouching there. Above us we heard another fusillade of cannon shells.

The helicopter made two more attacks, during the first of which there was a louder explosion that must have been the petrol tank of one of the scout cars going up. The explosions in the final attack were intermingled with shrieks of pain, and I guessed that some of the men taking cover in the opposite ditch must have been hit. Then the noise of the gunship's engine began to recede and when it had almost completely faded we cautiously moved out of our hiding place. The helicopter was still visible a couple of kilometres to the south, firing at some new target, but then it moved rapidly away in the direction of the heaviest gunfire.

Two of the scout cars were burning fiercely and a third had been blown to pieces, but the fourth proved to be virtually unscathed when the Honanese captain examined it. "We can pack in seven, maybe eight, but no more," he said, looking at Knox. There were nine of us fit to travel - Knox, McSkimming, their driver and radio operator, the Honanese and his two men, one of the staff officers, who had a wounded arm, and myself. There were three other survivors too badly wounded to be moved, and they didn't look as if they would live long, anyhow.

I saw an opportunity to escape from this nightmare, even though it carried a risk that might be almost as great. "I'll stay behind," I said. "I'm a neutral, so the English won't do me any harm. And I can look after these poor fellows," I nodded towards the wounded men, “until the medics come up."

"The English are more likely to shoot first and find out who you are afterwards," McSkimming objected.

"I'll be all right," I said briskly. "Your job's to get your chief away from here as quickly as you can, before another helicopter appears. It can't be very far now to Auchterarder."

Knox seemed to have subsided into a kind of torpor, and I don't think he noticed that I wasn't packed into the back of the car with the others. I caught my last glimpse of him as the car drove away, sitting hunched up beside the driver, his incongruous little head sunk low between his shoulders, his eyes staring vacantly ahead behind misted spectacles.

They left me some morphine and I gave it to the injured men, after I had done what I could to stop their bleeding. It was a relief to me, too, when the drug began to take effect and they stopped their terrible moaning. With garments stripped from the dead I covered them up against the biting wind that was beginning to gather strength.

I didn't have long to wait for the first signs of the advancing government troops. My view of the road was clear for nearly a kilometre back, and I was able to pick out the shapes of three rapidly approaching Tartar armoured cars. These I decided to let go past, since they would probably be looking for trouble, and were likely to shoot at anything that moved. So I lay flat in the ditch while they thundered by on the road above me.

A few minutes later two scout cars appeared, but I decided against trying to attract their attention because of the speed at which they were travelling. There were no fleeing Scots to be seen, and so I guessed that their retreat must have been cut off already - or perhaps they had taken to the hills.

After about half an hour I could hear as well as see the approach of a large number of vehicles, with two scout helicopters circling above them. I had made myself a white flag from a triangular bandage and this I waved at the approaching convoy. The armoured car that headed it ignored me and so did the first ten or twelve trucks, each of which was crammed with battle-stained infantrymen. But then a dispatch-rider on a motor-cycle pulled up at the roadside and started to question me in English. He didn't understand either my Japanese or my few phrases of halting English, but the sight of my Press card seemed to satisfy him and he roared away before I could point out the wounded men to him.

Groups of vehicles continued to thunder past for the next half-hour - more troop-laden trucks, armoured cars, half-tracks, gun-tractors pulling a battery of field guns, two self-propelled anti-tank guns, and still more trucks. Once I saw two ambulances approaching and tried to flag them down, but they drove on without stopping. One of the three wounded men had stopped breathing now and I closed the pale blue eyes that stared at me unseeingly out of his ash white face.

A little later, when the road was temporarily deserted, a large black bird came circling around and suddenly descended on one of the corpses that was lying about eight metres distant from me. I hurled a steel helmet at it and it rose into the air, screeching raucously, and flew away. No doubt it would return eventually to enjoy the spoils of war, but not while I was there to defend the dignity of my species.

Another convoy appeared in the distance, and as it approached I saw protruding from the fourth car a television camera on a tripod. At once I leapt to my feet and began to wave and shout, but to my bitter disappointment the television crew, who were Easterners, didn't slow down. They probably thought I was a survivor of some minor engagement wanting a lift.

I was standing on the grass verge, watching the receding television car, when a screech of brakes behind me made me jump, and I almost toppled backward into the ditch. A mud-spattered Rough Rider had drawn up beside me, and through the driver's window was thrust the round, red face of Bernie.

"Hello there, captain," he said. "Didn't expect to see you quite so soon. What are you doing here?"

"What are *you* doing here?" I croaked in delighted astonishment. "I thought you were in London."

"We were till the day before yesterday," he replied, "but then a little bird told me they were going to make the last big push up here, and she," he jerked his head backward, "wouldn't give me any peace till we came - see what I mean? Said you were bound to be around and you'd need the car."

At that moment I saw Miranda, getting out of the passenger door. She ran round the front of the vehicle, her long, black cloak streaming out behind her, and threw herself into my arms. As I felt the warmth of her body and her soft lips covering my cheeks with kisses I knew that I was home again.

CHAPTER 13

The climax of the great Festival of Peace was to be a mammoth parade and rally in Smithfield, a large open space in the northern part of London. The date had been chosen to coincide with the Christian holiday which the British call 'Easter' – inexplicably, because that was the name (so Miranda informed me) of one of their goddesses before they became Christians. The holiday actually celebrates the death and resurrection of the Christian god in his human manifestation, an event which they believe guarantees immortality to everyone who has been properly signed up as a member of his religion.

I had been waiting impatiently for the Festival to be over, because then I would be leaving for home and Miranda would be coming with me – to be my wife. I was still scarcely able to believe my good fortune. On that evening when Bernie and she had found me on the road I had asked her to marry me. I had asked her because I knew that until I did I would have nothing else to say to her.

She had paused for a long time before replying, and then she had said, "Yes. I couldn't bear the idea of not being with you – and I think that's about the only good reason for marrying someone."

In the weeks that followed I had been busy reporting on the mopping up operations in Scotland. General O'Neill had been insistent that there would be no taking of revenge, and for the most part his orders were obeyed by the English soldiers. Those that I encountered seemed genuinely shocked when they found whole communities ravaged by hunger in the bitter winter weather, and were happy to help distribute the food that came pouring in from Eastern aid agencies. Inevitably, some of it got wasted but, as far as I could see, only a comparatively small proportion.

A week after the fighting in which I was involved, which became known as the Battle of the Ochil Hills, O'Neill declared an amnesty for all fighting men who laid down their arms. There was a pocket of continuing resistance based in the Forest of Atholl, but hunger and extreme cold combined to bring that to an end about three weeks later.

Nothing further was heard of Knox until a rumour began to circulate that he was still alive and had escaped to Ireland. The Irish government firmly denied any knowledge of him; but then an official communiqué from O'Neill's headquarters stated tersely that he was "known to have fled the country with Angus Mackie and several other associates." Wherever he was, he was lying low.

I had begun making arrangements to travel back to Japan, with my Foreign Editor's agreement, when a surprising new development had made me change my plans. O'Neill announced the beginning of a process of return to civilian rule. In six weeks' time, he said, there would be elections for a Constituent Assembly, which would be charged with the task of drawing up a new constitution for Britain, to be implemented in the summer.

John Marlowe had been following the political manoeuvrings in London while I was in Scotland. He told me that O'Neill (who had been taught about the perils of military involvement in politics at our Staff College in Kashiwara) had struck a deal with Mark Gowrie, the youthful leader of the opposition People's Democratic Party. Gowrie was typical of the younger generation who had come into politics since Independence, and he was bursting with new ideas – chief among them a proposal for a new, federal constitution.

So, for six weeks Gowrie and his colleagues – who were not all youthful, and included a phalanx of grizzled trade union leaders who had played a notable part in the Independence movement – campaigned up and down the country. They advocated a federal Britain, made up of seven Cantons: North Scotland, South Scotland, North England, Middle England, South England, London Region and Wales. Each Canton would have its own Assembly to manage local affairs, and would send two representatives to a Senate in London, to protect its constitutional rights against any threat of encroachment by the National Assembly.

The surprise election campaign had caught the former governing party, the British People's League, in considerable disarray. Several of its senior members were in jail, awaiting trial for corruption uncovered with the help of Japanese investigators brought in by O'Neill. Its leader, John Serjeant, had fallen out of favour with the religious hierarchy because of a newspaper story revealing a past affair between him and one of his Cabinet colleagues, the aptly-titled Minister for Women's Affairs, Edith Groom.

This loss of favour among religious voters by the BPL may have prompted Gowrie to drop his party's long-standing commitment to a secular state, and include in the draft constitution a clause recognizing 'the special position of the Christian religion.' In his proposed Senate four seats would be reserved for the four Archbishops. As a result, the religious hierarchy had given its tacit approval to the People's Democratic Party's manifesto, and had snubbed Anne Cobbleigh's Christian Heritage Party, with its proposal for a theocratic state in which the Virgin Mary would have been proclaimed Queen of Britain.

The election had taken place just a week before the Festival of Peace, and had resulted in an overwhelming victory for Gowrie and his PDP. Immediately O'Neill had invited him and several of his colleagues to sit on the governing Council of State, and the transition to civilian rule had begun. There was an almost palpable mood of optimism as I made my way hand in hand with Miranda through the crowd assembling at Smithfield, towards the block of seats reserved for the media.

My own feelings of euphoria were redoubled by a telegram I was carrying in my pocket. It was from the *Nagoya Guardian* and said, "Miranda Medway winner of News Photographer of Year Award." When I had shown it to her at breakfast her face had been the face of a little girl on her birthday morning.

Our seats were in the front row of a stand next to the dais from which O'Neill was going to preside over the pageantry. Bernie and Marlowe were already in their places, and several other familiar faces came into view as we approached. Kakuei, the AP reporter, waved a cigar at us; and, much to my surprise, I found that the seat behind mine was occupied by the student I had met on the plane from Provence. I introduced him to Miranda and asked, "How do you come to be in those seats? Have you taken up a more ephemeral form of communication than the considered judgments of your thesis?"

He smiled and replied, "There's a magazine back home called *New Life Styles* that asked me to do a series on the psycho-sociological significance of events over here, so I got myself accredited. I'm interested in the kind of event we're going to see today – the orchestration by subliminal manipulation of the sub-conscious desires and frustrations of the masses. Here it's serving the interests of a ruling elite, of course, but in an autarcho-democratic society it can have a cathartic political role."

I heard a suppressed giggle from Miranda, and remembered that I had once recounted to her all the etymological details of my meeting with the student. "Have your views on violence and national self-identification been modified at all by what you've seen in Britain?" I asked him.

"Confirmed rather than modified," he replied. "The existential dynamics of the situation provide a classical example of the role of internecine violence in creating a predisposition to counter-revolutionary restructuring of governmental institutions in a manner likely to precipitate a confrontation between exploited and exploitative elements. I would prognosticate an authentic revolutionary struggle within a year."

"Who will the revolutionaries be?" I asked.

"The exploited masses, of course," he replied, "spearheaded by those members of the proletariat who have been given military training to enable them to participate in the late conflict with the northern ethnic sub-group. I would anticipate that initially they will find it expedient to form an alliance with quasi-democratic malcontents from among the former elite; but if the revolution achieves viability those retrogressive collaborationists will undoubtedly be eliminated."

"And what do you think will happen then?" asked Marlowe, who had been listening with astonishment slowly spreading over his long face.

"I would anticipate," said the student, "that you might have here in Britain the first authentic proletarian autarcho-democracy in the West, outside of the Slavonic People's Republic and North Greece."

"Do you still think that will happen if the military regime earns enough money from the oil to give everyone a little bit extra – and especially the soldiers?" Marlowe asked.

The student smiled condescendingly. "I would prognosticate that the oil revenues will not have attained to a significant level before the present rapidly escalating shortfall in world food supplies begins to make a socially disruptive impact on levels of consumption in this island, whose nutritional intake is heavily dependent on imported comestibles. But, of course, that prediction could be disauthenticated," he continued, "if there were to be an upsurge of pseudo-humanitarian sentiment leading to an indiscriminate distribution of grain reserves. I've just written an article for *New Life Styles*, warning progressive elements against joining in such sentimental clamour without weighing the inevitable political and socio-economic consequences."

"Have you been to Scotland?" Miranda asked him.

"No," he replied, "but I am sure the conditions of total nutritional deprivation described so vividly by your colleague in his paper must be acutely distressing. There would appear to be genuine humanitarian grounds for the application of immediate measures of relief, such as are now being implemented through the Union of Peoples. But in the long run it is difficult to envisage any fundamental reorientation of socio-economic structures which are semi-feudal unless it is preceded by total disintegration. The regime's current endeavours to expedite a return to normality seem to me to be a clear indication of its essentially retrogressive politico-societal stance."

Out of the corner of my eye I saw the student's fellow-countryman, Iguchi, approaching the stand. He waved when he caught sight of me. "Isn't that Shinroku Iguchi?" asked the student.

"Yes," I replied. "I met him in Scotland. We covered several events together. How do you come to know him?"

"I went to school with his son, Dorgon," he said. "I think the last time I saw his old man was at a New Year party at their house about six years ago. You said he was simulating the role of a journalist?"

"Simulating?" I queried.

"Yes," he replied. "Iguchi works for the Federal Intelligence Agency. Espionage in the interests of neo-colonialist expansionism is his avocation."

"That would explain several things about him that puzzled me," I said. "I ought to have realized. By the way, did you know that his son – your friend – had been killed in South Greece?"

A faint flicker of surprise passed across his face. "I was not aware of that," he said. "But we hadn't been in communication for several years. I have little doubt that he was a willing collaborator in the auto-destructive process of resistance to historical inevitability."

Iguchi was squeezing his way along the row towards us. "I've just heard a piece of news I thought you'd like to know about," he said as he approached.

"Oh, yes? What's that?" I asked.

"Knox really has gotten away to Ireland," he replied.

"You've heard the inside story, then?" I said. "How did he manage it?"

"It was a near run thing, by all accounts," Iguchi replied. "They'd caught up with him, just as he had a boat waiting to take him off from a little village on the island of Islay. That young fellow who used to show us around – McSkimming – held back the English soldiers from the end of the jetty with a sub-machine-gun till the boat got clear, taking Knox and Mackie with it. The navy tried to intercept them, but it must have been pretty impossible in the dead of night, and with mist on the water. Anyhow, they finally made it to Ireland. The government over there says it has no idea where they are, but I've heard for a fact that they're holed up in the Glens of Antrim. There's no way that the Irish are going to agree to extradite them."

"Did you hear what happened to McSkimming?" I asked.

"Oh, they gunned him down in the end."

"He deserved a better cause to die for," I said, sadly.

"Why is it," asked Miranda, "that the worst causes seem to provoke the fiercest loyalty?"

"Maybe it's because brave-hearted, muddle-headed young men like McSkimming start to have doubts about them; but they've been taught that doubting is a sign of weakness, and so they think they have to trample their reason under jackboots of blind obedience," I suggested.

"Well, I'd better be getting up to my seat. I guess that's the official party just arriving," said Iguchi. "Nice to see you again."

"Thanks for giving me the news," I said, as he edged himself out to the gangway.

A motorcade had drawn up and General O'Neill, accompanied by various dignitaries, was moving towards the dais. "That's the Archbishop of Canterbury," said Marlowe, pointing to a sharp-faced, bespectacled man in splendid, jewelled robes and a curious, pointed hat, who carried a tall staff with an ornate crook on the top. "He's the head of the religious hierarchy."

"He looks as if he's not in favour of anybody having fun," I remarked.

"He's new to the job," said Marlowe. "Must be a tricky time to take over, with the political situation so uncertain."

"Who are the others?" I enquired.

"Members of the new Council of State," he replied. "The young fellow with the big ears is Gowrie, and the bruiser beside him is his deputy, John Stanlow, who used to be head of the Union of Weavers and Spinners."

The official party took their places and a military band struck up an Eastern-sounding piece of music that I recognized as the national anthem. Everyone stood up and the flag, with its triangular segments of red, white and blue, was broken from the flagstaff behind the dais. Then the parade began. We had been told that the emphasis would be on peace and reconciliation rather than on victory, and certainly the military contingent, which headed the procession, was small. There was no mistaking the enthusiasm of the crowd, however, and the soldiers, sailors and airmen were cheered with almost hysterical delight.

Next came a series of floats bearing tableaux representing the island's history, from the raising of the ancient stone circle at Stonehenge to the departure of the Japanese on Independence Day. These were followed by contingents of citizens wearing their working clothes. There were miners in helmets, fishermen in oilskins, farmworkers carrying pitchforks, and many others. Last of all came the children, hundreds of them, smartly turned out in their Eastern-style school uniforms.

When they had passed the dais the children swung round and lined up along the far side of the arena. Then groups of youngsters performed folk dances and gymnastic displays, to the delight of the spectators, who doubtless included many of their relations. One group performed a dragon dance of the kind that used often to be seen in Japan when I was a boy, but which is comparatively rare today.

"That takes me back to my childhood," I said to Miranda. "You still keep some of the customs you borrowed from us. We always have dragon dances at the New Year."

"But that's not Eastern," she protested. "Look, there's the English patron saint, Saint George, coming to kill the dragon."

"It just goes to show that everybody has dragons," I said, putting my arm around her shoulders and hugging her. "Next New Year, if we spend it in Japan, I expect you'll find a lot of things to remind you of home."

She turned her head and looked at me with wide, brown eyes whose warmth was like summer sunlight on that chilly afternoon. "If you're there I won't need anything else," she said.

When the children had finished their performance they gathered themselves into a huge phalanx in the centre of the arena and sang a Christian hymn. Then the Archbishop went to a microphone on the dais and began talking in a language that I hadn't heard before. I remembered reading that the Christian priests still performed their ceremonies in a long-dead language of the old Roman Empire, which few ordinary people were able to understand.

As if she were reading my thoughts, Miranda whispered, "That's the old language that the priests use. It's called Latin."

"Do you understand it?" I asked.

"I had to learn it at school," she replied, "but I don't remember much of it. Oh, yes – I think I recognize this bit. It's from the Bible – the holy book. I had to write out a translation fifty times, for being late for chapel."

"Can you translate it for me?"

She squeezed my arm and said, "I'll try very hard. It's a bit about the end of the world, and how peace will come on earth, and God will judge people and rebuke mighty nations that are far away. They will make their swords into ploughshares and their spears into pruninghooks, and one nation will not raise the sword against another, and they won't learn about war any longer. But everyone will sit under his vine and his fig tree, and nobody will make them afraid, because the voice of God has said so. For everyone of the people will walk in the name of his god, and we will walk in the name of our God for ever and ever."

The Archbishop stopped speaking and the children began to

sing again.

"You did that very fluently," I said, hugging her. "It's a wonderful vision, but it would need a god coming down out of heaven to make it come true. There's a piece that's very much like it in the Buddhist Sutra of the Golden Light. The Buddha says that all the rulers of the earth will be happy and rich, and will never again invade each other's countries. They will learn that the smaller their desires the greater will be their blessings; and they'll free themselves from the suffering of war. And then their peoples will be glad, and the upper and the lower classes will blend together like milk and water. And they'll be sensitive to each other's feelings and work to increase the sources of goodness. The earth will be fertile, the climate will be temperate, and the sun, moon and stars will keep to their proper courses. There'll be no meanness in human hearts any more, and at the end of life great multitudes will go to swell the heavenly hosts."

"Oh, so Buddhists believe in heaven, too," said Miranda. "I suppose most people dream about the same things, whatever their religion; but dreaming doesn't seem to bring them any nearer."

"And yet, if we didn't dream we'd have no hope," I said, "and without hope I don't think we could go on. But does he," I nodded towards the Archbishop, "really believe in the dream he was reading about, or is it just a comforting incantation?"

When the children ended their hymn the Archbishop started up again. "He's saying a prayer now," said Miranda. "He's asking Mary, the Mother of God, to intercede for our country and give us a thousand years of peace."

The Archbishop was followed at the microphone by General O'Neill. "Now we're in for an endless political harangue, I suppose," said I, drawing her closer to me, and feeling the comforting warmth of her soft body.

But I was wrong. The General was terse and soldierly, stressing the need for national unity, calling for hard work all round, and dangling the prospect of an early return to civilian rule. At the end of his little speech he stepped down from the dais and, flanked by a couple of his aides, started walking towards the children. Immediately, a television crew rushed forward, followed closely by three or four photographers.

"This walkabout wasn't on the programme," said Miranda. "I

must go and get a last shot to complete the collection." She produced her camera from underneath her cloak. "It'll fit nicely in your autobiography alongside the one of Knox with his arm round you," she added, with a laugh.

I patted her bottom surreptitiously as she turned to leave the stand, and she smiled at me over her shoulder with a mischievous intimacy that made me long to be alone with her again. "Don't spend too long on it," I called after her. "We'll go to that inn near the hotel, the 'Cheshire Cheese', and have something hot to eat."

She ran gracefully, her cloak streaming behind her, to join the group that was gathering behind O'Neill as he made his way into the ranks of the children. Then, out of the corner of my eye I glimpsed another running figure, coming from the side of the stand. There was a shout and one of the policemen lining the perimeter sprinted forward to intercept him. Two more policemen came running from the opposite direction.

The man halted about five metres from O'Neill's party, pulled something out of his pocket and hurled it with an overhand action that sent it spinning in a steep arc. He shouted loudly as he threw the missile, but the only word I could make out was "Scotland".

There was a flash and a report as the grenade exploded, and then a spurt of grey smoke rose out of the middle of the crowd. I couldn't see Miranda any longer. With a surge of strength that I didn't know I possessed, I vaulted over the front of the stand and started running, cold fingers of fear clutching at the pit of my stomach. Children were screaming in shrill terror, and several small bodies collided with me as they ran frantically from the scene of the explosion.

Pushing between the photographers and television crew, I saw the general bending over the body of a golden-haired little girl in a bright red dress. His uniform was splattered with blood, and I suddenly realised that the dress was not red, but white. The crimson stain that covered it ended at a hem beneath which there were no legs.

Then I saw Miranda. She was lying almost at my feet, her arms and legs spreadeagled on the ground. Her eyes were wide open and they stared up at me, frozen in an instant of incredulity. Below her right shoulder a red stain was creeping across her yellow sweater. I heard myself utter a cry that was unlike any sound that had ever passed my lips before; and I sank to my knees on the ground beside her.

Pressing my ear to her chest I could hear no sound of a heartbeat. Frantically I tore back the ragged edges of the hole in her sweater, to reveal a wound that was four or five centimetres long.

"Try this to stop the blood, captain," said the distressed voice of Bernie from somewhere above me, and he thrust his grey woollen scarf into my hand.

I had unfastened her cloak and was trying to pass the scarf beneath her shoulder when Bernie spoke again. "The medics are here, captain. Better let them have a go. See what I mean?"

I stood up as two young orderlies in army uniform appeared behind Miranda's head, one of them already unwrapping a field dressing as he bent over her. Within a minute she was on a stretcher and being carried across the open space at a brisk trot.

"The hospital is just over there, by the trees," said Bernie, as the agitated crowd opened up to let the stretcher-bearers pass through.

"Let's go with them," I said, looking into his face for some sign of encouragement. Tears were streaming down the contours of his round, red cheeks, and in his brimming eyes I could see no sign of hope.

We followed the stretcher-bearers.

CHAPTER 14

Bernie and I sat side by side on a hard bench in the ante-room of the hospital's new operating theatres wing. At least Miranda was still alive. I consoled myself with that belief, confirmed by the tall, flaxen-haired nurse who had seen her as she was rushed through to the doctors. And Bernie, too, had recovered his composure and was now trying to reassure me.

"They have some clever fellows here, captain," he said. "Trained in Japan – a lot of them. They'll get her through it. I'm sure they will. Lucky it happened right beside the hospital. She won't have lost too much blood."

"Is it a good hospital, then?" I asked, wanting to be reassured.

"About the best we've got. It's the oldest one, too. Started about eight hundred years ago by some rich fellow who got religion. They say he was travelling in Italy when he got sick and this saint appeared to him in a vision and told him he'd get better if he built a hospital when he got home to London. So he did; and he called the hospital after the saint – Bartholomew. Leastways, that's the story I've heard. I expect he was feverish when he thought he saw the saint, but it was a good thing for people in London that he did."

"Eight hundred years ago?" I said. "That's about the time we were having some bad civil wars, like the one you've just had here. It was a bad time in mainland East Asia, too. Funny how one thing reminds you of another. Some poems I learnt at school – they were written around that time by a woman called Li Ch'ing-chao. She lived in what's now Shantung, and her husband died during a big war with the Chin. She used to write poems and send them to him when he was working away from home. After he died she wrote some beautiful verses. They weren't so much sad as breaking through to something on the other side of sadness."

"I know what you mean, captain," said Bernie. "There comes a time when you've got to get a grip on what's happened and start again. I know that's how it was with me when the wife died."

"I didn't know you'd been married," I said; and I thought with shame how little I had troubled to find out about this man, who had been such a loyal friend to me and to Miranda. "When did she die?"

“Eight years ago, next Yom Kippur. It was the cholera, the big epidemic. You see it happening to other people but you never think it can happen to you. One day she was rushing around, holding everybody else together, like she usually did. She took in my brother Eli’s kids because his wife had caught it – though *she* got better. And the next day the cholera had her. There was nothing they could do. I knew when they took her to the hospital it was all over.” Tears glinted in his eyes at the memory.

“I’m sorry, Bernie,” I said. “It must have been a terrible thing to go through.”

“It just about knocked me out, captain. First thing, I wished it had been me that the cholera took, instead of Miriam. But then I thought that would have been no different, because I’d still have been parted from her.

“I’ve never been a religious fellow, and all that stuff the rabbi came across with didn’t do anything for me. But I did remember something I’d read at the synagogue classes I’d had to go to when I was a kid. It’s in one of our holy books, and I thought at the time the fellow who wrote it had a better idea of what really goes on than a lot of those prophets and other fellows, who were always up in the clouds. I’ve a good memory for what I want to remember, and it came back to me when I needed it.

“This fellow said there’s one thing that will happen to everybody, whether they’re good or bad, clever or stupid. They’ve all got to die. And if you’re one of the ones who’s still alive then at least you’ve got hope. ‘A live dog’s better than a dead lion,’ he said. The ones who are dead are nothing. So if you’re still alive you ought to be happy and enjoy your food and drink while you can. And whatever you have to do, do it with all your strength, for there’ll be no work, nor anything else, when you’re in your grave.”

“Not bad advice,” I agreed.

“It made me think that weeping and wailing couldn’t do Miriam any good; and meantime Eli’s kids needed attention. We didn’t know then that his Hannah was going to get better. So I got on with it. And later, when I had time to think again, I worked it out that what Miriam would have wanted would be for me to make the best of whatever bit of life was left to me. That was the one thing I could do for her, in a way. But really it was myself I had to do it for. We can’t keep the dead with us and it's no use pretending that we can."

"No, but I hope today it's the living we're going to keep," I said, looking anxiously at the closed door, with its scratched and dented green paint and its panel of glass at head height. That was to prevent people in a hurry from colliding with one another, I speculated; but it seemed a very long time since anyone had come through that door.

I reached into my jacket pocket for my notebook, remembering how I had made Miranda start using her camera that day in Newcastle, when she first saw a dead body. As I turned over the pages to find a blank one on which to begin my report I thought about photographs. The editor would be wanting me to wire a photograph of her if the story was going to lead with… for a moment I refused even to think about the word… to lead with her death. The faces of fellow-journalists crowding around the hospital door until they were pushed away by soldiers rushed back into my memory. One photographer had even taken a picture of me. Because of Miranda I was part of the story and no longer just the story-teller.

In the past year I had seen people killed and maimed, bereaved and homeless, and I had felt horror and sympathy as I wrote about them. But in spite of my sympathy I had been detached from their suffering, an outsider looking in on their tragedy and recounting it to others who couldn't see it for themselves. Only now had I become involved in what was happening. If Miranda were to die that single death would mean more to me than all the others put together.

I realized then just how much I needed a measure of detachment in order to do my job properly. But maybe that was because I believed that my job was about presenting the facts as truthfully as I could, taking account of the limits on my own observation and knowledge. There were a lot of people who wouldn't agree with my definition. They would say, wrapping it up in the jargon of whichever ideology they happened to embrace, that I ought to be committed to a political objective and report only those facts that would help to convince my readers of the rightness of that objective.

So, what had happened to Miranda could be presented in such a way as to demonstrate what dastardly scoundrels the Scottish rebels were or, alternatively, it could be presented as proof that the British military government's oppression was leading to an endless cycle of bloodshed and resistance. Either way Miranda would serve only as a pawn in the ideological power game.

As I began to write the report – *At today's Festival of Peace in London, celebrating the end of the civil war in Britain, an attempt was made to assassinate the leader of the military government, General O'Neill* – I wondered whether everything I was doing and had done wasn't just a futile waste of time. Of course the readers couldn't be expected to care about, or even to be more than marginally interested in, the suffering of people so remote from their own experience. The idea that they should all feel as deeply about every distant death as I would feel about Miranda's was just a bait devised by moralists to lure us all into their labyrinth of endless guilt. Maybe there was a level of concern that was appropriate to each situation, and if we fell below it we were callous, but if we tried to rise above it we were only being sentimental.

What I wanted more than anything at that moment was to be able to put those thoughts to Miranda, and to hear her softly voiced opinion, cool and sensible, as I had heard it so many times when we were driving along in the Rough Rider, or when she was lying close in my arms at night. The memory of those nights flooded over me and I couldn't go on writing.

The door opened and the flaxen-haired nurse came in, followed by a stout, bald-headed man in dark green overalls, wearing rimless spectacles. The nurse was smiling. I stood up, feeling a tightness in my throat as I struggled to hold in check the optimism engendered by her smile – the fear that I might not be able to cope with disappointment was almost palpable.

The surgeon spoke to me in heavily-accented, careful Japanese. "She is going to be all right. The splinter did not hit anything vital and I was able to remove it without causing any further trauma. Here it is." Triumphantly he held up between his thumb and forefinger a shard of metal about two centimetres long and one centimetre wide.

"There was also some concussion from her fall, but it wasn't serious. She seems to be a healthy girl and with rest she should soon recover from it." His serious expression changed to a smile and he added. "It is not always I am able to give good news. She was very lucky."

"I am sure that she was also lucky to have had the benefit of your skill," I said, extending my hand to him in the Western fashion. "Without it the news might not have been so good. Thank you – and thank your colleagues for me too, please," I added, turning my head to acknowledge the nurse. Then, remembering what the alternative news might have been, I began to cry.

I hadn't forgotten our old, imperial tradition of not revealing one's emotions in front of the natives, and I was glad to feel liberated from it. Britain is a country unencumbered by such traditions, and my three companions were unembarrassed by my tears. The surgeon shook my hand warmly, the nurse hugged my shoulder and Bernie, who also had tears on his cheeks, exclaimed, "It's the best news ever, captain. I told you this was the top hospital. See what I mean?"

I asked if I could see Miranda, but the nurse said it would be better to wait until next morning. She was in Intensive Care, but if she had a good night she might then even be able to talk to me. So Bernie and I left the hospital and got on with the business of sending my report.

He had rescued Miranda's camera and he took the film to be developed. When the prints came back the last picture was of a fair-haired little girl, her face shining with eagerness and excitement, reaching out towards General O'Neill. I recognized that happy, hopeful face as the child whom I had seen a few moments later with her legs blown off.

Bernie and I were back at Saint Bartholomew's Hospital early next morning. Taking a short cut across Smithfield, we picked our way through the litter left uncleared since the previous day's aborted celebration. At the hospital gate there was a small posse of armed soldiers and we were halted. Bernie ascertained that Mark Gowrie had arrived, attended by two television crews, to visit the injured from yesterday's incident – four children, a teacher and Miranda.

My press card and Bernie's eloquence in a discussion with the young lieutenant in charge eventually gained us admission. It took us some time to discover where Miranda was located and Gowrie's visit was over by the time we reached the foot of the stairs leading to her room. His party was coming down as we were about to go up. (I later learned that Matron had firmly refused to admit the television cameras to Miranda's room.)

"Mr. Gowrie, I'm from the *Nagoya Guardian*. May I have a word?"

He was wearing an Eastern-style sweater and slacks, and he smiled broadly as he stopped at the foot of the stairs and held out his hand to me. "Good to see you. I've just been talking to your brave young woman. I've seen some of her photographs, you know. Terrific."

"Do you think that yesterday's bomb incident will be a set-back for the peace process in Scotland?" I asked.

"No. Not at all." He looked into my eyes with a very serious expression. "What you've got to understand is that ordinary, decent people in every part of this country have come to realize that there is no alternative to unity. If we're going to survive in a world of globalisation we've all got to be pulling in the same direction. The action of some deranged fanatic – and we've got to accept that there may be more than one of them – is not going to deflect this country from its chosen path. What we're looking for now is the help of our friends overseas to get things moving again economically. This country has enormous potential, and those who become our partners in development now will reap huge rewards in the future, not only for us but also for themselves.

"I hope your colleague will soon be taking pictures again. And don't forget about us, now that Britain has stopped being a war zone. Good news may not be as exciting as bad, but I'm sure your readers will want to know what happens next."

He raised his hand in a kind of benediction and trotted towards the door, followed by two gun-toting soldiers, a harassed-looking young man who was probably his secretary, a hospital administrator and the two television crews. Bernie and I went upstairs and found Miranda with a face that was drained of colour but able to glow with happiness the moment she caught sight of us. I felt that my future had been restored to me.

It was four weeks before the doctors were satisfied that Miranda was ready for a journey half-way round the world. By then the weather had changed again, as it does so often in Britain, and the sun was setting in a clear sky against a backcloth of crimson when we boarded the plane at London Airport. It was rising in a mist of gold over the

Sea of Japan when we completed the last lap of our journey.

We never did return to Britain, in spite of our best intentions. Miranda's mother, Eleanor, came to live with us in Kyoto, where we settled when I became a freelance. And the photographs of Japan, and later of East Asia, that Miranda took with the fresh eye of an outsider soon became so popular that her work was constantly in demand.

Some twenty years after the British civil war I had an idea for a working project that would have involved us both. By that time Britain had become firmly established as one of the West European 'Young Bull' economies. My plan was to write a series of articles, illustrated by Miranda, on how the change had been brought about, and what the lessons might be for other developing countries. I was hopeful that, if I reminded him of our encounter on the hospital stairs, I might even be favoured with an interview by Mark Gowrie, now white-haired and nearing the end of his fourth period as Prime Minister.

I took the project to the *Guardian*, for which I still occasionally did work, in the hope that they would agree to publish, and to pay the costs. Initially there was a good deal of enthusiasm, and I was invited to meet the Foreign Editor to discuss the details. However, from the moment I sat down in her paper-cluttered office (the cyber-revolution seems to have done nothing to reduce the volume) it was apparent that there were going to be problems. Asked to outline my 'thematic proposals', I began by recounting the statistical indicators on which I had grounded my research – reduction in infant mortality, improvements in literacy, nutrition and longevity, and, of course, the massive surge in Gross Domestic Product.

"Those are not the indicators I've been looking at," she said, briskly. "Inequality is what you need to concentrate on. They're growing a big, ugly middle class – even sending their kids here in droves to our universities and business schools. Foreign companies are making whacking great profits; and the peasants are deserting their traditional communities and flocking to the towns to work in factories and mines – not to mention the ecological damage that's being done to their wonderful countryside. They're watching Eastern television and losing their own ancient culture. I hear they even have two Taketomo Fast Food Bars in London. And, of course, they're falling into the tourism trap. Have you heard about the child prostitution in a place called Brighthelmstone? Those are the things I'd want you to concentrate on. That's where you'll find the lessons that other countries might learn while they still have time."

I didn't agree. She was buying and I wasn't selling. I made my excuses and left; and so we've still not been back to Britain. But we do have one continuing contact. An early recruit to the ranks of the rapidly expanding middle class was our old friend, Bernie. When long distance air travel became cheaper and adventurous tourists began to trickle into Britain he was quick to offer his services. From a modest beginning with a single coach he soon expanded into package tours, and eventually into hotels and restaurants. (One activity in which he always maintained a personal involvement was a 'Tour of the Civil War Battlefields'.)

Bernie's burgeoning prosperity has enabled him to make an annual visit to Japan, combining business with pleasure. So every year we look forward to spending some time with him, and hearing his perspicacious comments on the latest developments in the Land of the Setting Sun. And every year he brings some beautiful and unusual gift for Miranda.

This year he presented her with a rectangular package in glittering golden paper and watched her unwrap it with the eager anticipation of a schoolboy in his round, red face. Inside was a box containing a perfect replica of the Rough Rider, about twelve centimetres in length. Miranda exclaimed in delight as she took it out of the box, and Bernie said, "Made in Newcastle upon Tyne, that was. New factory, making toys for the export market. It's a joint venture between a local fellow, called Armstrong, and the Yamamoto Corporation."

"Why did they decide to copy the Rough Rider?" I asked. "It's been out of date for years."

"Ah yes, captain, but that adventure film, *Samurai Spaceman*, is still going the rounds on television, and the kids love it. You remember, they used a Rough Rider in it to chase the villains across the Gobi Desert?"

"I remember it," said Miranda. "It was on the telly here last New Year. But that one was painted bright yellow, like the picture on the box, and yet this one is dark green, just like our old faithful."

"By special request," said Bernie, grinning broadly. "Mr Armstrong owed me a favour."

I took the little vehicle from Miranda's hands and examined it. "All it needs is a bit of mud," I said. "Funny how we eventually forget about the mud, and yet I seem to recall that you were always fighting a losing battle against it."

"That's the way it is, captain," said Bernie. "Your memory has a kind of filter, to get rid of the things you want to forget about. If a fellow's filter isn't working properly he can have bad nightmares."

"I suppose it's the same with history," said Miranda. "Countries forget about some of the things that happen to them because they don't want to remember, and sometimes they remember things that didn't really happen."

Bernie scratched his balding head with a rapid, scrabbling movement of his fingers. "I guess that's right," he said. "Some things are best forgotten; but it's not a good idea to forget about the mistakes you make. If you've had a bit too much to drink and you fall into a ditch on your way home, you should try hard to remember where it was. Otherwise you might fall into it again one night, and the second time you could break your neck. See what I mean?"

www.ingramcontent.com/pod-product-compliance
Ingram Content Group UK Ltd.
Pitfield, Milton Keynes, MK11 3LW, UK
UKHW041945190726
13854UKWH00004B/1803